Cardinal Sins
T.B. Wittkofsky

TBW

Copyright © 2026 by T.B. Wittkofsky

All rights reserved.

No portion of this book may be reproduced in any form without written permission from the publisher or author, except as permitted by U.S. copyright law.

Contents

1. Red Carriers   1
2. Red Couriers   40

Red Carriers

The winter the cardinals started tapping on the glass, the town learned to keep the curtains drawn.

People said the birds were omens.

Old wives' talk, dressed up with new certainty. My neighbor, Mrs. Darrow, taped black felt over every pane and told me she slept fine. I could tell she lied. She had the look all the newly frightened wore.

Dry lips.

A slow turn of the head with every sound.

We all felt watched.

The first tap came to me on a Tuesday. Three sharp knocks on the kitchen window. I set the kettle down and went still. Frost starred the corners of the glass. Outside, a cardinal sat on the sill like a drop of blood that chose to perch.

A male.

Red from beak to tail. He cocked his head. He tapped again.

"You have the wrong house," I said. It felt foolish to talk to a bird, but many of us did. It felt worse to say nothing while it asked to be let in.

I turned back to the kettle. The third knock came, softer than the rest. I did not look again. I made my tea, hands steady, and carried the mug to the table. When I glanced up, he was gone. The little smudge of heat he left on the glass faded to nothing.

By evening, the town had a new loss.

News moved faster than the plows. A boy from the blue house by the creek. Asthma, they said. The family had never told anyone. The boy's mother cried in the grocery store vegetable aisle and apologized to the lettuce for dripping on it. By nightfall, our street had two new pieces of black felt and a sign on the blue house door.

Please call before visiting. Thank you.

The cardinal came again on Wednesday.

Tap.

Tap.

Tap.

He brought a feather this time. I watched it stick to the edge of the sill as if the cold had learned to pinch. I kept the window closed.

On Thursday, nothing came.

I slept.

I woke feeling guilty about the sleeping.

On Friday afternoon, after a morning of dead calls, slow emails, and a lunch that tasted like paper, the cardinal returned. He brought the feather inside this time. I found it at the base of the back door, where a draft worked in winter. The feather had a darker tip. Almost black. I looked for an opening in the seal, found none, and placed the feather on the table.

I told myself I would throw it away.

I did not.

I know a red bird can be just a bird. But the year in the middle of my life, loss rearranged the furniture in my head. It left silence in places where there had been music. That year, a cardinal rode the fence behind the hospital and watched me hold my husband's hand as he slipped out of what his body had become. It watched my mouth shape his name. I did not cry until the cardinal flicked its tail and flew into the evening. It left a single feather on the hood of my car. I kept it in a book I never finished.

People said cardinals were messengers.

A sign that someone was visiting.

People said a lot of things to make grief less bare.

I did not mind the talk. A story in the mouth takes the place of a scream.

This new feather weighed almost nothing. You would think weightless things could not harm anyone.

Then you remember paper cuts and words.

I tucked the feather into a jar beside a coil of twine and a few screws. The cardinal had taken to waiting on the telephone wire. He switched from foot to foot and sang three notes. He watched me watch him. I tried to go about my chores.

Salt the steps.

Fold the towels.

Wash the pot with the burnt rice and tell myself it would come clean if I did not hurry it.

The bird sang again.

The doorbell rang.

I flinched and almost laughed. It felt like a prank the universe would enjoy.

On my porch stood a woman I did not know. Thirty, maybe less. She had the kind of face that would be called kind in a eulogy. She wore no hat. Her hair held little needles of snow.

"Are you June?" she asked.

"Yes."

"I'm Bella Morgan," she said. "I think your bird is mine."

We both glanced at the wire. The cardinal beat his wings, then settled.

"I work at the State Office," she said. "Field Division Two. We call them ferrymen. It is not official. It is just what the old files call them. The cardinals that knock. They come when there is a crossing."

"What do they ferry?" I asked.

She stepped closer as if she needed warmth from the answer. "Sometimes grief. Sometimes the person. Most times part of the one left. The payment varies."

"You think I owe something."

"I think he picked you," Bella said. "And yes."

I thought of slamming the door and saying I was busy. The laundry, the dishes, the broken hinge on the cupboard that always fell off. None of it had kept anyone alive. Work does not offer absolution, only distraction.

"How do you know he picked me?" I asked.

"He brought the feather inside. They do that when they are ready. May I see it?"

I could have said no.

I brought the jar.

Bella held the feather like a match she would not light. "This kind," she said, "asks for a memory."

I pretended that did not make sense. "Memory of what."

Bella took a breath. "It is always the same kind with this shade at the tip. The black means it takes your memory of a name."

I stood very still.

The house knew the weight of silence. It settled onto our shoulders like another quilt.

"I do not want to give up any names," I said.

"It only takes one. The one you bring to the window when you open it."

"I do not plan to open it."

The cardinal tapped once as if to correct me.

Bella's eyes softened. "I tell people, and they think I am a thief for the State. I am not. I am a mourner who got a job."

"Why the State?"

"Because patterns belong somewhere," she said. "And because some doors need a file number. It makes people feel better to sign something."

"I am not signing."

Bell nodded. "You do not have to. He will wait. They do not tire."

"He will freeze."

"They do not freeze," she said. "That is part of it. That is why the old folks called them ferrymen. They belong to a place on the water where it does not matter if cold exists."

"Purgatory," I said.

Bella did not answer.

We stood together and watched the bird. He made no move to leave. He made no move to enter. The wind crossed the yard and erased the old footprints.

"Who would I get back," I asked, "if I opened the window."

"You would not get anyone back," Bella said. "You would only stop hearing a name. Sometimes that is enough to let the days go by. Sometimes it is an act of betrayal. No one can decide for you."

"There is nothing in exchange."

"There is nothing in exchange," she said. "Except a little quiet."

I poured tea because hands like tasks. I did not offer her any. She did not ask. We were strangers the way grief makes you kin.

"Who did you lose," I asked.

She looked at a spot on the floor as if she could read the stains. "A husband," she said.

"Did you open the window."

"Yes."

"Do you regret it."

"I do not have the word to regret," she said.

I waited.

It took me a long breath to understand what she meant. She had lost the name, and with it went the shape of the grief. She could feel its size but not its letters.

"Some people find peace," she said. "Others only find a blank spot they press, again and again, like a bruise they cannot name."

"Why come here then?"

"Because the ferryman we tracked came to you. Because someone should witness the act. Because some people change their mind when another human stands by."

I set my cup down and went to the window. The cardinal hopped closer. I could see the fine black whiskers at the base of his beak. His eye looked wet; It reflected my face without mercy. The old feather in the jar seemed to hum.

I tried to summon any name but the one the bird would take. I thought of the boy in the blue house and the lettuce in the store aisle and the sound of my own voice in the hospital. I thought of the way his hand had cooled, finger by finger, as if his body had a list it checked off before leaving.

I lifted the latch.

"Wait," Bella said. "You can keep the window shut and still live. You know that."

"I know," I said. "That is the hard part."

I raised the window two inches. Cold poured in like a blow. The cardinal did not enter. He waited.

I said the name out loud because I could not let it leave me without hearing it one more time. I said it again. The sound fell into the space between glass and air. The cardinal dipped his head. He lifted one foot. He set it down. The name left me like breath. It did not go with drama.

It just went.

I shut the window.

Bella watched me. "Can you say it again," she asked.

"I can't," I said.

"What do you feel."

"I feel like the room lost a color," I said. "I feel less heavy. I hate that I feel relief."

She nodded. "There is no correct feeling."

We sat at the table. The kettle clicked as it cooled. The jar with the feather seemed old now, like a toy from a house where no child lived. The cardinal remained on the sill for a long time. Then he hopped to the wire and sang a flat little run of notes that sounded like a lullaby without words. He flew off over the field and into the line of bare trees.

Bella left without asking for anything. She gave me a card with a number on it. It had no name, which felt fitting. If I called, someone would answer as if they had been waiting for me all day.

That night, the house felt like someone had moved the furniture again. I walked the rooms and tried to imagine how they had looked before. I tried to picture the face that went with the missing sound. I could remember the shape of a hand and the warmth of breath on my neck in summer. I could remember a laugh that rose quicker than mine. I could not fasten the right word to any of it. My mind skittered over the blank like a skate on clear ice.

I slept without dreaming.

In the morning, three new pieces of felt went up on our street. People like to think they can hide from a pattern.

Weeks passed. The cold held. The river rimmed with ice, then thickened. The ferrymen knocked at other houses and waited on other wires. The State sent more people like Bella to witness and answer questions that could not be answered.

I did not call the number. I told myself there would be no point. I told myself many things. I kept the card in the junk drawer where elastic bands went to dry out and batteries lay uncertain about their future. I opened the drawer more often than I needed to and learned the way the card's corner caught on a crack in the plastic organizer.

Word moved through town like water finds a low place. Stories bubbled up in the pharmacy line. In the post office where the heat worked only in the morning. On the church steps where smoke did what prayer could not. You could map the arrivals by the fabric on windows.

Black for those who chose to stay whole.

Gray for those who were thinking.

Red for the handful who wanted the ferrymen to see them and come quicker.

There was a man named Johnny who hung red cloth. He drove the salt truck and sang along to old songs with the windows down no matter how cold. He had a daughter who worked the night shift at the nursing home. His wife had left long ago, or had died, or had never existed. The versions disagreed, and people did not press him to clarify. He wore a hat knitted by someone with small hands. It kept a dent in his thick hair long after he took it off.

Johnny said to anyone who would listen that he wanted to forget the man who had run the old green light and bent his mother's life into a shape pain likes. He wanted to forget that name because he had said it in court and in his own kitchen and into the dark when pain made him a different sort of animal. He said the name still tasted like metal even after all these years. He hung red cloth and kept the window unlocked. The ferryman never came for him.

"It is not a wishing well," Bella told me later when I asked. "They do not work on spite. They come when loss chooses you, not when you choose loss."

I did not know if that was mercy or cruelty.

I saw Bella again a week after the first visit. I was carrying salt to the steps. She was coming up the sidewalk with a folder tucked under her arm. Her coat looked thin. She had a way of walking that said she liked to arrive half a second before she was expected.

"May I come in," she asked.

I stepped aside.

She wiped her boots on the mat like a well-trained guest. She set the folder on the table and did not sit until I sat.

"How are you," she asked.

"Lighter," I said. "Wrongly."

"I understand."

"Do you remember her name," I asked without thinking. "Your sister."

Bella's mouth twitched. "No," she said. "I remember the shape of her. She had a scar in the middle of her forehead from running into the corner of a table when we were little. It made a pale line that caught light in photographs. I remember her taste in music and the way she smelled like shampoo mixed with pencil shavings during exam weeks. I remember the winter she fell through the creek and we ran home with our jeans stiffening in the wind. I do not have the small sound that held all of that together."

I looked at the folder. "What is in there."

"Old things," she said. "You asked about purgatory. You were not the first. The State likes a paper trail, so they dug until they found something that looks official. Mostly, it is letters. Church newsletters in counties where the weather makes people sentimental. Notes from a doctor who thought this was a sleep disorder and wrote about it for a small journal no one read. A copy of a poem someone printed in the year nineteen sixty something and left at a bus stop. We have more paper than answers."

"Why bring it to me."

"You opened a window," she said. "You will be tempted to open another. It helps to see the pattern other people made with their choices."

She spread the contents out.

Small clippings.

A page typed on a typewriter that liked to catch the bottom of the e.

A photograph of a window with frost feathers rising up the pane like someone had held a fern against the glass and prayed.

I picked up a sheet that looked like a church bulletin. There was a line about a bake sale. A list of people who had fallen ill. A brief paragraph near the bottom.

The Advisory Committee wishes to remind parishioners that the birds at the window carry holy purpose, not malice. If you do not wish to accept their service, close the curtains and recite the chosen psalm. If you accept, do so in a spirit of humility and understand the loss you purchase will arrive marked and unreturnable.

"'Unreturnable'," I read. "As if it were a dress."

"People try to send things back," Bella said.

"What happens when they try?"

"They talk themselves in circles until they wear a groove their thoughts cannot climb out of. They call me and hang up. They call me and cry without words. Some of them decide what was taken was a sin and they want to atone, so they make themselves hurt in other ways.

Hunger.

Cold.

Silence.

It does not put the name back. It just adds weight."

In the stack there was a photocopy of a journal article with the title cut off. The word ferryman appears in handwritten ink above a paragraph about dream states. The author had observed three subjects who reported visitors they called red carriers. The subjects described a sense of lifting pressure upon waking. Two of them could not remember a specific word they had used to say every day before the visits began. The author concluded that memory is an organ that bleeds quietly and then scabs if you let it.

"You like this author," I said.

"He died young," Bella said. "His family put his papers in a box and never answered letters from our office. We make do with what we can steal from library copy machines and people who keep everything."

I thought of my own drawer.

The card.

The rubber bands.

The batteries with no plan.

"You said I would be tempted to open a window again," I said. "How many times can a person open before they are a house with no door."

Bella folded her hands. "Some people open once and feel they have sinned against themselves, so they never touch the latch again. Some open once and feel clean. Some open twice and go very quiet. A few open three times and learn to live like people underwater. They move slow. They keep their hands out in front of them in rooms they know by heart."

"Why three?"

"Because there are three kinds that come," she said. "You met the first. He takes the small word that holds the person together in your mind. The second takes the knowledge that you gave up the word. She makes a smooth surface over the act. And the third takes your talent for seeing the dead in the living world. He closes the trick your mind plays when it wants to talk to what it cannot have."

I thought of waking in the night and seeing the shape on the edge of the bed that was not there when the light came on. I thought of the way steam on a mirror can look like handwriting when you wish it to. I thought of the old feather in a book and what I had turned it into.

"I met the second," I said.

Bella's face sharpened. "When?"

"Yesterday. She tapped once and waited. You reached my door as she reached the rail."

"And?"

"I closed the latch."

Bella sat back. "Good."

"Is it good?"

"It keeps you honest with yourself," she said. "It keeps the bruise visible."

The town did what towns do with a slow disaster.

It made rules.

The City Council met twice and released a statement that asked residents not to feed the ferrymen. It used polite words and asked us to be mindful of the birds' purpose. It asked us to report doorstep gatherings to a hotline. It asked us to avoid gatherings of mourners that could block traffic. It attached a sheet of resources

Grief counseling.

Heating assistance.

Contact information for the State Office, Field Division Two.

A new phrase appeared.

Window rites.

People lit candles, wrote names on slips of paper, and burned them in bowls bought for soup. They put the ashes in corners and told themselves they had made an altar. There was a house that cut out all the panes and left nothing but frames. They said it was "an art installation about transparency." Then they wore gloves and hung plastic sheeting on the first wind and slipped a space heater into the kitchen and called it "a statement of endurance."

There were people who made money. A man sold small glass cardinals with holes in their backs for cinnamon oil. A woman stitched window covers that were prettier than black felt. She used fabric with tiny red birds, and people laughed, then bought them. The hardware store put a display of latches in the front and a sign that read:

Take precautions.

Most days, the latches were gone before lunch.

I took a day to walk by the river where the old mill used to stand. The ice made a sound like someone was cracking a knuckle far below. I followed tracks that could have been a fox. They led to the cattails and then to a place where a cardinal perched, female, brown, her crest sharp against the white. She watched me but did not knock on any part of the day. I watched her and tried not to give her my act.

On the way home I saw Johnny on the salt truck. He and I waved, and he shouted through the open window that the music was for the birds, because if you sing to anything long enough it will think you are its kin.

I saw Mrs. Darrow fighting with a piece of felt that refused to lie flat. I went to help and she let me. Her hands shook in a way that belonged to every season. It was the shake that comes when a person realizes time is not a river but a deep bowl, and you can fall from any edge into the middle.

"You opened," she said.

"How do you know?"

"I can hear it," she said. "Your voice sounds like a house with a rug pulled up."

"My voice always sounded like that."

"No," she said, and smiled a little to soften it. "It sounds like you stepped around something instead of through it."

"Will you open?" I asked.

She looked up at her own window as if it might speak. "I lost the father I had and the father I wanted in the same year," she said. "One died. One finally told me he could not be the man I needed. I can say both names. I do not want to lose either. They sit together on my tongue like a pair of mismatched chairs. It looks wrong. It fits me."

We finished the felt and stood by the mailbox while the wind tried to read our pockets. She asked if I wanted stew. I said "yes" because grief likes company that puts bowls on tables and does not ask for answers. We ate in her small kitchen and when the spoon clinked the bowl she made a sound that might have been a laugh or a swallow. She told me about a newspaper boy who used to throw the paper at her steps and always hit the rail. She said she had fancied him a poet until he grew into a man who ran a pawn shop and never read anything longer than a receipt.

When I left, a cardinal sat on her gutter and watched us say "goodbye."

He did not knock.

We did not invite him.

Bella called me the next morning and asked if I would come to a meeting. She said it would help to hear how others shaped their days after. She said the State Office was trying not to be the enemy, and a room with chairs was a way to start.

The meeting was in the basement of the library. The carpet smelled like mildew that had been told to behave. A table held coffee, paper cups, and small cookies iced to look like cardinals. I watched a woman bite the head off one and look ashamed as if the cookie had feelings. Bella stood near the door and nodded at me as I came in. I counted ten people, then twelve, then fifteen. We sat in a circle because that is what circles are for.

Bella did not lead.

She sat and listened.

A man in a sweater with holes in the sleeves asked if anyone had ever opened the window three times and lived to tell the tale. A woman with paint on her jeans said her grandmother's sister had. She said the old woman had become gentle almost to the point of cruelty. She smiled at everything and could watch a house burn without a change in her face. She said the woman did not cry when her dog died. She said it became hard to tell if the grandmother's sister was a saint or had simply forgotten what the world was for.

A young person with a ring through one brow said they had opened once and now could not look at their mother because everything their mother said sounded like a room without furniture. They said their mother had not opened but sounded like someone who had. They said they felt like the ferryman had traded places and they did not know who to charge with the crime.

There was a nurse who said she had never opened and did not plan to. She said she liked her grief with edges. She said it made her careful in ways that kept people alive. She said she had told this to her husband and he had said she was selfish, and she had told him he might be right. He had opened and he had started sleeping in a chair because the bed no longer made sense to him. She said she would sit in the chair with him sometimes and they would hold hands like people on a slow train.

When it was my turn, I said a name and lost it. I felt relief I did not like. I said I could remember the shape of a laugh and the weight of a hand and the line of a jaw and could not summon the small sound that tied it all together. The man in the sweater nodded as if I had named a pain he had watched from across a parking lot. Bella wrote nothing down and asked nothing. I liked that. It felt like a room where language could rest without being made into a list.

After the meeting, I helped Bella fold chairs. She said she knew the cookies were a mistake but had not known how to stop the volunteer committee that liked to make everything festive. I asked if the State Office had a policy on festivity. She said policy was a word that tried and failed to pin a butterfly to a board without damaging it.

I said I had thought about the second window again. She nodded and said "of course". She asked if the female had come back. I said no. She said sometimes they visit in sets. Sometimes they test a latch by tapping once in the morning and once at night to see when a person is weakest. She said the third kind comes at dusk because that is when imaginations are long and light is short.

"Do you want the third to come?" she asked.

"I do not know," I said.

She studied my face like a map. "When I was a child," she said, "I liked to stand in doorways. One foot in the kitchen. One in the hall. My mother used to tell me to pick a room. I think I took this job because I never learned to pick. I like thresholds."

"Is that what this is," I asked. "A threshold."

"Yes," she said. "And a ferry."

The blue house by the creek put out a stack of casseroles on a table by the door with a note.

Thank you. No more food.

It became a place where people left other things. A book of psalms. A scarf. A small carved bird that was not a cardinal but looked enough like one to count. The mother came out sometimes and rearranged the items as if they were letters and she was trying to spell a word with no vowels.

I met her once at the end of the street. Her name was Lydia. She had a voice that made you think of the way quiet can be warm. She asked if I had opened.

I said "yes."

She nodded like a scientist collecting data. She said people liked to tell her to open and lose the name so she could sleep. She said she did not want to sleep. She said sleep had become the only place the boy's voice had the weight it needed to stand upright.

I said I understood.

I did not.

Not in the way she meant. Each grief holds its own shape like a secret language you can guess at and never quite speak. She said the ferryman had come to her kitchen once and she had watched him tap and had not moved. She said the sound had become a metronome in her blood. She said she could stir soup in time to it and wash the counter and fold a towel and find that she was still alive after all that. She said there was a kind of wrong that felt like breathing.

We walked together to the corner where the mailboxes leaned like old men. She asked what I had lost the name of.

I told her.

She said the name aloud as if to check.

She said it again.

She smiled sadly when I did not react. She said she would hold it for me until I wanted it back. She said nothing returns, but there are ways to keep something near by saying it for someone else. I wanted to tell her she did not owe me that. I wanted to tell her she owed herself the right to say only her own names for a while. I said thank you because small words are the only ones that can carry certain weights.

I woke one night to tapping that was not at the window. It was inside my chest, a small patient sound like knuckles on a door. I went to the kitchen and stood by the sink and did not turn on the light. The room was a shape I knew by heart. The fridge made its old humming complaint. The furnace coughed once as if clearing its throat before an apology. Outside, the yard looked like it had been erased and drawn again by a child who liked straight lines.

The cardinal was on the sill.

The female.

She did not tap.

She waited the way a person waits when they know they will be invited in and want to spare you the shame of asking too quickly.

I stood with my fingers on the latch and thought of not only my own act but the acts of every person who would sit in that library room and sip coffee and cry into cookies. I thought of Bella standing in doorways. I thought of Lydia holding a name for me as if it were a small animal and needed warmth.

I did not open.

I lifted my fingers away from the latch the way one lifts a hand from a stove.

Slowly, with a respect that looks like fear.

The female turned her head and her eye caught the reflection of my face, giving it back to me. She flew to the wire and sat there as the sky learned to be morning.

In the days after, I found my mind testing me. It would say.

Remember the sound you lost? Remember the act you did not perform?

My mind is a dog that likes to bring things to the door and ask if it can come in with them. I pet it and tell it to lie down. Sometimes it obeys. Sometimes it chews the leg of a chair.

The State put out a pamphlet. It had diagrams. A cardinal on a sill with labels.

Crest.

Mask.

Bill.

The arrows made it look like a machine. The words were meant to soothe.

They did not.

There were sections on safety and consent and reporting. There was a paragraph on fraud that made me laugh in a way that felt like coughing. *Who would impersonate a ferryman*, I wondered. Then I imagined someone tapping on a window to make a person open it and lose a name for no reason other than harm. The pamphlet did not have space for that picture.

Bella said the pamphlets came from higher up and she kept them in a closet so she didn't have to look at them. She said sometimes a boss would ask how many pamphlets had gone out, and she would make up a number that sounded reasonable and then say she had recycled the remainder to save paper. She said they liked that answer. She said saving paper made grief look green.

We talked, more and more. She told me the way her sister had gone was not clean. There had been a rope and a letter and the kind of mourning that makes you think a person could be forgiven for thinking the world would offer no more, not even one small kindness.

She said she hated that word, forgiveness. It pretends to be a gift and is just a mirror. I said I had forgiven things that later grew back like weeds. She said she had forgiven the rope because it did not know it was a weapon. I said I had forgiven a hospital bed for holding what I could not. We both agreed we did not know what we meant and liked saying it anyway.

She came to my house on a Sunday with a bag of oranges and a blue notebook. She said oranges were for winter and the notebook was for a project. She asked if I would help collect the stories that did not fit the forms.

Not a study.

Not a report.

Something like an atlas drawn by children who know where the sun goes and cannot put it on a map.

"What would we do with it?" I asked.

"Keep it," she said. "Hide it if we have to. Bring it out when someone tries to make rules that hurt. Show it to people who think they are alone."

"Will it change anything?"

"It will change the shelves in one closet," she said, and smiled. "We start small."

We took down words as if they were birds that had flown into the house and needed to be carried gently out the door. We wrote the day and the exact time. We described the sound of taps and the weather and what the person had eaten for breakfast if they remembered. We asked if there had been anything that broke in the house that day.

A lightbulb.

A plate.

A zipper.

We asked if the ferryman had been seen by a neighbor or only by the person waiting at the window. We asked what was given and what was received and if the person felt the exchange was fair.

People told us things they had not told anyone. A woman said she had opened and given the name of her brother who had hurt her and had slept for three days without dreaming and had woken in a room that looked bigger and had thought she had made a mistake and then had thought she had saved herself and then had thought both at once and had learned to make tea without choosing between the thoughts.

A man said he had opened but whispered the wrong name on purpose because he did not think the ferryman had the right to choose, and nothing had happened, and he had felt foolish and then angry and then sad at his own small attempt to make the universe pay attention.

A child wrote that the bird looked like a crayon drawing and that their mother had told them to go to their room and they had and they had put a blanket over their head and hummed and none of that had changed anything.

We put the pages in the blue notebook and kept it in my house because Bella said it felt wrong to keep it in a building with a flag. She said flags are for the living and this felt like a place where both kinds of people came and sat without saluting.

The third ferryman arrived at dusk in late February as the sun tried not to set and failed.

I heard him before I saw him.

Not a tap.

A scrape like a dull knife across a dry board. I knew before I turned that the evening had moved into the room. He was larger than the first. Or felt larger. The red on him looked old and new at once. He sat with an intent that made me think of a person who had practiced waiting in a field for a fox to show itself.

He did not tap.

He watched me.

The space filled with the ache you feel when you try to remember a face you saw in a dream. I placed my hand on the latch and felt my arm understand my mind. It knew what it was to open. It knew the weight and the movement and the brief release of cold. I asked myself who I would be without the trick my heart played when it needed to survive a day.

No scent in a coat. No shadow on the wall that looks like someone you love pausing in a doorway to think of a joke. No soft conversation with air.

I thought of Bella's sister. I thought of Lydia's boy. I thought of Johnny and his red cloth and the man in the sweater who wanted legend more than comfort. I thought of Mrs. Darrow's two chairs. I thought of the blue notebook and the way it had started to smell like oranges from Bella's bag.

I did not open.

I whispered to the glass. I said, "I will carry what I have. I will give it shape when it tries to flatten me. I will not make myself smooth to move through this world. I will be rough where I need to catch and hold."

The third tilted his head. If he had been a person, he might have smiled. He flew to the wire and stayed past dark.

Bella came that night without calling. She stood on my porch and looked at my face and knew. She sat at my table and took an orange and peeled it in one long curl. She set the peel on the table in the shape of a river and we looked at it as if we could trace a way out.

"Tell me a story," she said.

"About what?"

"About the person whose name you lost. Use the world around the name. Make it hold."

So, I told her about the day the water pilot light went out, and we could not find matches and how we had laughed wet and cold and called the neighbor and he came over with a lighter held like a magic trick. I told her about a splinter in a thumb and how we had carried it like a broken promise until it pushed itself out one morning at breakfast and we felt like saints. I told her about the way a song on the radio once came on at the exact moment it had to, and we had looked at each other and felt like the world had been made for us for one second, and then we had known the world was made and that was enough.

Bella cried quietly and wiped her eyes with the side of her hand the way a person does when they have done it often and do not want to make it dramatic. She told me about the creek. How the ice looked like skin. How her sister had always walked on the edge of things. How she had liked to hang one arm off the bed and touch the floor with her fingertips while she fell asleep because she liked to feel grounded. How Bella had found the letter and had not read it for a week because she wanted to leave one door unopened in a house where all the doors had been forced.

We ate an orange each and left the peels on the table like a map we were not done with.

Spring came late like a guest who wanted to make sure we understood our manners. The ice left the river and the sound it made was like applause in a hall. People took down the felt, and pretended it had been a choice they wanted to make.

The ferrymen grew rare.

We said we had survived something and then pretended we had not said it, because to say it felt like an invitation for it to return.

I planted herbs in a pot on the porch and felt like someone who could feed herself small things. Bella took the blue notebook and made a copy that she put in her freezer, wrapped in a plastic bag to keep the pages from smelling like meat. She said freezers are the safest places because no one steals from your frozen peas. She said a boss had asked where she kept her files and she had pointed to the cabinet, and the boss had been pleased, and the cabinet had held only pamphlets and a jar with three dead flies.

Lydia came out without a coat one afternoon and we stood in the weak sun and let it work. She said the boy's bed would be turned into a place to put folded blankets because you have to put something somewhere. She said she had started to say his name in the morning, each morning, into a cup of coffee, and then she would drink the coffee and feel like she had taken a sacrament of her own making. She said sometimes she said the name of my lost one too. She said she did not know what she was doing and liked that.

Johnny painted his salt truck even though he did not own it. He painted a thick red line along the side and a small bird at the front near the headlamp. The town told him to remove it, and he said the paint was arterial and could not be scraped and they said that was not how paint works and he shrugged and left it.

The man in the sweater cut the sleeves off when the weather warmed and took up running around the school track. He ran at dusk when the third kind used to come and he ran with his head down as if he were lowering himself through something heavy like honey.

The woman who had bitten the head off a cookie started making cookies shaped like latches and people bought those too. I could not tell if we were a satirical town hidden away in North Carolina or a southern hospitality one that takes pride in the silence.

Maybe we were both.

Summer taught me a new way to count time. It gave me a bench in the park where I could sit and watch a pair of cardinals feed each other and pretend that I was not making that into a message.

It gave me storms that made me pull plugs from sockets and sit on the floor like a child with a blanket over my knees. It gave me Bella at my table listening to stories we did not know we had kept. It gave me Lydia laughing for the first time since I had met her. It gave me Johnny singing to a new song that had no words. It gave me the man in the sweater taking a break and drinking water and looking at the sky as if he could learn something from it that did not change.

Bella and I drove to a town where an old woman had written a letter to the State Office in three colors of ink. The letter said there had been cardinals in her windows since nineteen fifty-one and no one had believed her and now everyone said they had seen them, and she did not know whether to be angry or to be pleased that the world had caught up. She said she had opened only once. She said she had kept the other kinds waiting until they got bored. She said boredom is a weapon. We sat in her kitchen and ate pie, and I asked if she could teach me how to be boring to grief. She said it takes practice and very little makeup.

We visited the graveyard on a hill where snow would have been pretty if it had been winter. It was summer and the stones looked ridiculous in the sun. Bella put her hand on a stone and closed her eyes. I did not ask if it belonged to her sister. I did not want to make that into a rite. She told me later it did not. She told me later she touches random stones so that people do not look at her and think she is a woman with a single wound. She said she is a woman with many small wounds that make a pattern like a city seen from the air.

We passed a farm where a boy had set up a stand that sold lemonade and drawings of birds in crayon. He had drawn cardinals with blue wings and said the colors were wrong on purpose. He said the blue is the part you cannot see that does the work. He said the red is for the eyes. He poured us lemonade and asked if we wanted sugar and we said yes, he shook it in an old jar, handed it to us, and we drank it and thought of the buried work in everything.

I wrote a letter to myself. I put it in the book with the old feather and forgot it and then remembered. The letter said.

You took a word out of your mouth and kept eating anyway. You learned that hunger is not only for food. You found that relief can be an insult and a mercy at once. You decided to let some part of you keep dreaming even when it hurt. You kept the latch closed the second time. And the third. You may change your mind. You may not. Either way, you are the only witness you need.

It felt like the sort of letter someone would tell me was self-help. I put it back in the book and left it there like a stone at the edge of a path.

In autumn, the ferrymen grew bold again. They came at odd hours and to new streets. People newly moved in learned the local weather and how to buy felt. The council met in the basement of the church and talked about zoning as if it were a way to write a spell. They passed a measure that made window coverings a permit issue. The town did not comply. The measure died in a drawer with a broken handle.

A woman drove through, stopped at the diner, and asked if this was the place with the birds. The waitress told her it was and that she could leave now if she liked. Then the woman laughed like someone who had not been asked to leave a place in some time and said she would stay for pie. She ate two slices and then bought one to go and I watched her through the glass and wished her luck with whatever the flock would make of her.

The blue notebook grew thick. Bella bought a second and we called it "the second drawer." We started to index things lightly: Names with no vowels to stand for what we could not hold; Dates; Weather; A line about whether the person had a pet, and if so what kind. Dogs were common. Cats less, but there were some. A woman had a parrot that mimicked the tap, and she had to move the parrot to the garage for a month because it kept making her think the ferryman had come again. She felt cruel and then she felt practical and then she felt like a person with a parrot in a garage and she said it made for better parties.

I added to my own entry without telling Bella. I wrote that I sometimes thought I could feel the outline of the missing word in my mouth like a tooth my tongue checks when it is not sure if it is loose. I wrote that sometimes I think I hear it in crowd noise or traffic. I wrote that sometimes I wake with it in my throat and then swallow it away. I love and hate that there is a second when it feels near.

Winter again.

The second in this new pattern. The first snow came early and made everyone pretend to be surprised. The ferrymen did not arrive with the first flake. They waited like they did last year for the weather to become something you can name.

We were better at the rituals. We had learned how to refuse with kindness and how to accept with ceremony and how to sit with our hands on our knees and not move at all. Bella said the State Office had shifted from panic to boredom, which is the dangerous middle state where rules are made. She said pamphlets had become a program, and programs had become a budget, and budgets crave numbers and numbers crave bodies. She said she was tired of data that counted and wanted data that weighed.

She had started to use words like "we" in rooms with flags and words like "us" in rooms without. She looked tired but also like someone who had found the right tools and was not sure if she had the right hands.

"We have a case."

That is what Bella called it before she apologized for using the word. A man claimed a ferryman had taken something without consent. He said he had dreamed the window open and had woken with the sense of a loss he had not chosen. He said the State owed him a name. Bella and I sat with him in a room with a table and a plant that had learned to want little. He told the story three times.

First angry.

Then bored with his own anger.

Then in a voice that made me think of a boy who had been taught not to cry at school.

The ferryman had come to his dream and he had opened the dream window and said a dream word and woken with lips dry and a word missing that might have been the word for his father.

Bella asked if he wanted us to teach him how to make peace with having lost something he could not prove. He said "yes and no." We taught him how to stand in the kitchen in the dark and let the room hold him. We taught him how to say the word morning before it became a day. We taught him that wanting proof is a kind of grief, that it will not rest until it is fed, and you cannot feed it anything except time.

He left with a brochure he did not want and a phone number he would not call. He wrote to us a month later and said he had decided to keep a plant alive, and it felt like a lie he could live with.

I learned to look at cardinals without feeling tested. Sometimes I failed. The male would land on the fence and I would imagine he had a paper in his beak with instructions from a place that never runs out of tasks. The female would sit on a twig like a small, perfect machine for deciding. I would breathe and stay where I was. I would name the objects in the room and let my chest loosen.

Table.

Cup.

Window.

Bird.

Loss.

Love.

Quiet.

I started saying other people's names out loud in the morning and leaving the kitchen with them in the air like small ships.

Lydia's boy.

Bella's sister.

The man who had run the light.

The neighbor's mother who forgot how to tie her shoes and never learned again.

The names settled somewhere, I hoped. The house felt full of a presence that did not have to belong to me to make sense.

One evening in late January, the first cardinal came back. I knew it was him because of a small notch in his tail I had not noticed before and now felt sure of. He tapped once, then looked to the side as if he could see into another house where someone else was deciding. I stood and looked at him and said, "Not today."

He blinked once and stayed.

I said, "Not today," again.

He tapped in a rhythm that felt like counting.

I said, "I will not buy another quiet." He flew up and left.

I sat at the table and laughed a little and then cried a little and then ate toast because bodies like salt and heat and the sound of a knife on a plate when the world has tried to make everything soft. The toast had gone cold. I ate it anyway.

I dreamed of a room with no windows. It was not dark. It had light that came from a place I could not see. The walls were painted a color I could not name because the name had been a small word for a kind of blue and I had given it up long ago. There were three chairs. One red. One brown. One red again. The two red chairs were not the same. I sat on the brown. It was sharp and kind at once. A bird landed on the back of my chair, looked at me, and opened its beak and a sound came out that was not a word but did a word's job. I woke with my heart standing up in my chest.

I told Bella about the dream and she said dreams are rooms the ferrymen cannot enter without you. She said that is why some people fear sleep. She said that is why others love it. She said if a ferryman wants to bargain in a dream, it must learn your rules there. She said she sometimes meets her sister in a place with light and they talk about shoes because shoes are as safe a topic as any when the dead have no feet.

There is an end here, and there is not. The ferrymen do not pack and leave. They do not tire and choose a new town. They do not die and leave nests with small bones.

They come when they come.

We decide when we decide.

We carry what we carry.

On some mornings, I hear tapping and it is only a branch. On some evenings, a flash of color crosses the yard and my heart trips in my chest. I live with both states.

The knowing.

The unknowing.

The red that is a bird.

The red that is a symptom.

I open the curtain when I can bear it. I close it when I cannot. I talk to the glass and listen to my voice as if it belonged to someone I might meet in a store.

Sometimes I say the names I have kept and feel them sit up straight and look at me, ready for school. Sometimes I say nothing and let the house hum. Sometimes Bella calls and asks if I want to drive to a town where someone has written to say a bird has learned a new rhythm and they want to know if that means a new kind of loss. Sometimes I say yes. Sometimes I say no. Both are correct.

Lydia's boy is a smile I see in the corner of my eye when water boils. Johnny sings to the truck and the truck answers when it wants to. The man in the sweater with no sleeves runs in snow with his breath streaming like a banner he never meant to carry. The woman with the parrot brings it back into the house and the parrot has learned to sing the cardinal's song and now the woman wakes at three and thinks she lives on two roads at once.

I do not open the window.

I do not swear I never will. I have chosen my threshold and my ferry for now. I stand where a person learns the weight of the quiet they bought and the price they refused to pay. I hold my own name in my mouth not because I fear losing it but because I like the way it tastes when I am the one who says it.

When winter comes again and a ferryman sits like a small red question on the sill, I will go to the glass and rest my hand on the frame and think of every story in a blue notebook and every orange peel laid like a river on a table and every person who learned to make tea in a room with a closed latch, and I will speak to the bird as if it were a friend I respect and do not trust.

Not today, I will say.

Or yes.

Or wait.

And the cardinal will do what it does, which is to be the shape the world gives it. I will do what I do, which is to be the shape my losses have made that still fits through my doors.

The winter after the ferrymen learned our names, a real pair took the fence behind my kitchen and made it theirs.

They were easy to tell apart once I bothered to look daily. The male was red like a recipe you do not share. The female had that warm brown with a faint flush on her crest, a softer color that asked you to come closer. They came to the same post near the apple tree, always from the north, always just after the light found the edges of the field. They swapped seeds, the neat beak-to-beak pass that looks like a kiss from across a room. I tried not to turn that into meaning. I failed most days.

Bella said, "these are birds. Not ferrymen."

I said, "they wear the ferrymen's faces."

She said, "the living and the work of death borrow the same uniforms sometimes."

We had a name for their spot before long. Their spot, as if the yard could belong to anyone in winter. The fence post with the shallow crack and the flake of old paint that lifted when the sun hit it. He would land first, then she would arrive in a line of flight that curved like a thought finding its shape. They sat and watched me watch them and did nothing that would look strange to a person who had never met a ferryman. That was why I liked them. To share a fence with creatures who owed me no bargain and wanted nothing but seeds and a place to stand. That felt like a kind of rest.

The ferrymen still worked the town. People opened or did not. We got good at food and chairs and small sentences that could hold friends upright. The State Office learned to sit with its hands folded and promise nothing. Bella kept the blue notebook and put another in her freezer and once mailed a third to her own mother with a note that said, "keep this as if it were soup." Her mother mailed it back with cookies in the box and a line that read, "I am not good at soup but I am still your mother."

In that season I walked less and watched more. I found that the body learns to stand still the way it learns to move, with practice. I stood at the sink as the kettle worked and counted from the time the sun touched the far trees to the time the birds arrived at their spot. It was not reliable, but it felt like counting breaths. Some days they did not come and I learned to wait without inventing a story to punish myself.

The female did not come on a Tuesday. A thin cold had set in that made the air taste like a key. He landed on their post and called. That clear two-part tune.

Cheer, cheer.

The second note shorter. He waited. He called again. He hopped to the apple branch and back. He cocked his head as if he could see through time and find the shape of her against yesterday's sky. He did not leave for a long while. Then he flew east and tested every perch along the fence as if each might open into another yard where she was waiting.

She was not waiting anywhere that day.

I told myself she would come tomorrow. Birds go. Birds get pulled by wind and the quiet magnets that live under rivers. You learn that when your life is stitched together by movements you cannot control. I fed the kettle. I salted the steps. I wrote in the notebook. The word absent sits in a room without furniture. It does not help. It does not hurt. It does not sit.

Wednesday, he came, called, waited, and left. Thursday, the same. Friday, less calling. He sat, then he went to the arbor and back. He ate a seed without sharing. It looked wrong in a way you only notice after you have watched a pair enough times to see how they arrange their days.

The neighbor's cat brought an impossible amount of snow into his prints and shook his paws as if the ground had insulted him. He watched the post and the bird and did nothing because even cats know when to leave certain rituals alone.

I walked the yard with my eyes, not my feet. I did not want to find a small shape under the holly. I did not want to find the sign of a wing on the fresh snow that says a hawk has been here and done what the sky asks. I did not want to find anything that would make me step into a role for which I had not dressed. I did not want to bury a thing.

Bella came by in the afternoon with oranges and the kind of bread that forgives you if you cut it wrong. She stood at the window with me and watched the male land and leave and land again.

"Nature does not organize itself for us," she said. "But sometimes it chooses an angle that feels personal. That is the worst kindness."

"Do ferrymen die?" I asked.

She folded the orange peel in half and then in half again. "I do not know what they do when we are not looking. The State does not have a form for that."

"What do birds do when we are not looking?"

"They do work," she said. "That is why we call everything 'work' now. We like to feel aligned with something. They move their bodies through a world that makes no apologies. That is their act of faith or their habit. I cannot tell which."

On Saturday I found her. Not the ferryman. The bird. The female. She lay under the low yew by the back steps, where snow had melted last in a little cave children would have crawled into, had there been children here. She looked parked. Not broken. As if she had landed and decided to stop. The brown of her body looked warmer for being still. The red on her crest was clearer up close, a wash of color like a blush that meant nothing outside the small world of birds and what they do to find each other.

I said her aloud and it was not a name they could take. It was a description. Female cardinal. I said it again, to be sure I could form the words. I do not know why I needed to. Maybe because I had given up a name once and had learned to fear the edges of language. Maybe because I liked the sound of saying a thing exactly as it was.

I did not call Bella first. I went inside and took a small trowel from the closet and a paper towel and a shallow box left over from a pair of shoes. I lined the box and brought it to the yew. I spoke to no one and to everyone. I said, "here." I said, "forgive me if this is not the right place." I said, "you were alive and now you are not and this yard is less." I put my hands around her in the way you put your hands around a stopped clock: careful; respectful; simple.

Her body was both nothing and everything. Weightless until I lifted her. Then the fact of her rested in my palms as if I had been meant to carry her once before and forgot. I laid her in the box and closed the lid halfway to shade her and set the box on the porch while I cleared a small place along the fence where the earth remembered the sun.

Johnny saw me from the truck and walked up with his hat in his hands. He knew without anyone telling. He had the kind of face that can arrive in a moment like this and not make it his. We did not say her name because she did not have one for us to keep. He took the trowel and widened the small hole I had started and I held the box and thought of every body I had touched like this. Small ones. Adult ones. Names in my mouth or gone from it. He stepped back and I lowered the box and he pushed the earth in like a man who knows how to cover what the world asks you to cover.

"Do we mark it?" he asked.

"Not with a stone," I said. "She did not belong to ground. She belonged to branches."

He nodded. He went to his truck and came back with a length of red twine. He tied it around the fence post where they sat. A small cord, the sort you would use to fix a parcel. It looked right. It said, here, without pretending to explain.

The male returned that afternoon and sat on the red string and called the cheer he knew. He tilted his head. He hopped down to the exact slice of wood where her claws had always left their faint lines. He looked at the yard like a person looking for a coat in a closet where they live alone.

I watched him and felt a tightness on the left side of my chest. A small knot that had nothing to do with bargain birds and everything to do with the work of a heart that had been asked to be both an organ and a shelf for the breakables.

I made tea.

I did not drink it.

I placed my hand on the frame of the window and pressed. It felt like the wood could remember every winter and every palm.

The ferrymen came to the town less for a while, as if even their work had seasons. The living birds came as usual. Not always as a pair. The male visited daily and tested every perch as if he could force the past to line up with the present through repetition. I thought of liturgy. I thought of people who sit in the same pew long after the priest changes. I thought of Bella, who wrote, and of Lydia, who spoke her boy into coffee each morning until the cup grew light in her hand.

Bella asked if we should send a note to anyone about the female. I asked, "to who?" She said, "to the part of me that will try to make a symbol out of a death that does not need the weight I am tempted to put on it." I said, "yes, send a note." She wrote on a card. *Your bird died. The sky does not owe you a lesson. You owe the yard kindness.* She slid it across the table to me, and we both looked at it as if it were a toy that might break if someone breathed too hard.

Lydia came with a small bunch of dried grasses and wove them into the red twine on the post. She said the boy would have liked this because he liked to fix what was already working. Johnny sang all the verses of a song I only knew the chorus to. His voice was thin but steady and he kept the tune even when a gust pushed the sound flat. Mrs. Darrow stood with her hands folded like a prayer and whispered two names in alternating order. Both her fathers. She did not open the window. She never did.

You think, in a winter like that, that the universe will stagger the pains it sends. It does not. It can set them side by side, like plates on a table where guests you did not invite arrive and sit with their coats on. The knot on the left side of my chest came and went. Some days it turned into a line that ran to my jaw and down my left arm, a thin ache like a string pulled too tight. I told no one. I took small walks to the fence and back and promised myself I would tell Bella and then told her only a part, the version of the truth that can stand in daylight.

The female ferryman knocked once in late March. A quiet tap that did not insist. She sat on the sill and waited with that sharp head tilt that belongs to birds who know you are looking and do not care. I put my palm flat and could feel the cold through the glass. I had kept the latch closed twice for her and once for the third. I kept it closed again. She watched me with interest and none at all. She flew when the light slid and took the shine with it.

I thought of opening for her one last time and losing the memory of my act. That would smooth the floor under my feet. That would help me stop measuring the shape of my silence. I kept the window shut because grief is also the map that tells you where you are when the lights go out.

I wrote letters to no one. I wrote lists. Salt. Bread. Oranges. I wrote down sounds I loved in case words left me, the way some people fear sight will. The kettle. The furnace cough. The sudden hush when a storm stops. The whistle of the male when he sees the crest of the roof and knows he is nearly home.

Bella and I worked the notebooks like a pair of clerks in a shop that sells what cannot be priced. We added a page for animals found. Not a study. Only a record. We wrote, *female cardinal, found under yew, buried near post, red string*. We wrote the weather. We wrote who came. We did not write what we felt. That belongs somewhere else.

One morning in April, I woke with the feeling that the house had leaned in the night and decided to make a new shape of itself. Doors open differently when that happens. The air sits higher. I made tea. The male took his place and sang. I stood too quickly and my field of sight went gray at the edges and came back in a slow ring. I sat and counted my breath. Four in, four out. The little school of tricks you keep in your pocket for when your body forgets its lines.

Bella found me after lunch, because she had planned to come and I had not canceled. I had not called because the phone looked like too much language. She looked at me and put her hand on my wrist and made a face that people make when they decide which sentence helps and which sentence only cleans the speaker's conscience.

She said, "I am here."

She did not say, "you are not well."

She did not say, "you will be fine."

She made a call and a woman with calm shoes arrived. She took my blood pressure and listened and told me to get in the car because there are things that are better checked and timing is not a god but it likes to be honored.

I stared at the window. The male sat on the post. He turned toward me when my chair moved. This is my last clear picture of the yard from that day. The red string. The fence. The bird. The small line of damp earth near the post that settled in after winter and never fully dried. Bella said, "shoes," and I put them on. She said, "coat", and I shrugged into it, though the sun had changed. She said, "keys," and I followed her hands with my eyes as if she were braiding a child's hair.

The drive was short and long at once. Clinics are buildings that want you to believe in order. Bella held my hand while they threaded needles and asked for numbers. A nurse said, "you are brave."

I said, "no, I am here."

She nodded. "That is the right sentence." They put my body in machines that find things and said I would stay the night if I would. I would. Bella went to my house to get things. The kettle. The mug with the chip. The book that holds the feather. She promised to feed the cat we do not have. We laughed. The worst jokes keep blood moving.

I do not know if the rest of this belongs in my mouth. It can live in the mouths of others. There is a point at which the telling needs a different voice because the one that started the story has stood long enough and wants to sit.

Johnny said he knew something was wrong when the truck hit a patch of old salt and kicked it up. All the while at the same time, a cardinal whistled the two-note cheer and then added a longer phrase, a little flourish I had not heard him sing. He says he does not believe in signs. He says he believes in roads and the truth they tell you when you have driven them long enough. He says the road to my house had that quiet a road gets when the people inside the houses are looking at the same spot on their floors.

He says he knocked and waited and then let himself in because Bella had called and said, "stay with the house." He says he looked at the cup on the counter and the spoon near the sink and the red string on the post outside and felt a weight on his shoulders that he put there with his own hands. He says he walked the rooms and spoke my name to be sure the walls would answer if there were any answer to give. The answer was a kind of hush.

He says the afternoon cut into its own shape and sat. He says he brewed tea he did not drink and put bread on a plate and left it. He says the kettle sings even when it is not working because it has learned to be alive whether or not there is flame. He says he did not open the window because the ferrymen were not the kind you need for this work.

He says it became dark and then not, the way early spring manages light. He says the male came to the post and sat and did not call. He says he went to the window and they looked at each other like two men at a bar who recognize the same loss and decide not to talk about it. He says he put two fingers to his lips and whistled the song he uses to make the salt truck feel less like an empty building. He says it is only three notes, then two. A call he learned from a radio and forgot the words to. He says the bird answered with the old cheer and then, as if he had been waiting for this exact kind of human noise, adjusted the phrase and matched Ellis, three then two. They went back and forth until the small muscles in Ellis's mouth ached and the bird shook his feathers and looked satisfied like a man who has made it to the end of a shift.

He says Bella came back late, shoes quiet, mouth set. He says she went to the bedroom and stood in the doorway and did the private math that tells a person what to do next. He says the call came in the night and confirmed what the house had already said. He says after, he went to the window because the world tells you where to put your body when something breaks, even if it cannot fix it. He says the male cardinal was there, on the post, and the two of them whistled a small tune across the glass until morning found the red string and made it shine.

Bella says my face was peaceful. She says people always say that and most of the time it means nothing. She says this time it looked true. She says it looked like I had come to the end of a sentence and put a period down with care. She says she put the blue notebook on my table and turned to the last page I had written and ran her finger over the ink as if touch could add a line that the pen had not. She says she called Lydia, and Lydia came, and the three of them sat at the table while the kettle clicked and they did not drink the tea because they did not want it to be the last cup I had boiled.

They tell me the ferrymen did not knock. It was not their work. Or it was and they had learned a new schedule. They tell me the living bird came to their spot and sang the song they had built together out of feeding and waiting and sharing. They tell me Ellis whistled until his breath turned white and then stopped and then began again because sometimes you need to make a noise simply to show the world where the opening is.

This is how the town tells the next part.

They set the kettle on and boiled water for guests. They put food on plates. They spoke my name in the morning into coffee because that is how we live with names here. Lydia said it with her boy's. Bella said it with her sister's nameless shape. Ellis said it in the workshop behind his small rented house where he keeps tools that belonged to no one and everyone. Mrs. Darrow said it at the mailbox in a voice she uses when talking to cats.

They went through the old motions that keep human hands moving between the heartbeats that try to stop. They entered my notes into the blue book. They added a line. Female of the house, died on a Thursday in spring. They did not write a cause because they do not know how to make those words behave. They wrote who came. They wrote that the male cardinal kept the post and the string and adjusted his song to match a human whistle for one long hour.

Johnny kept coming by the house to straighten what did not need it. He fixed the cupboard hinge and put the chips from the mug in a small jar as if they could be seeds later. He swept the porch not because it was dirty but because the rhythm helped. He stood at the window when the light was right and put his fingers to his lips and sent a line of notes to the field. The cardinal answered when he liked. There is no contract between men and birds.

Only practice.

Bella took the orange peels from the bin and made them into ribbons on the table the way I used to. She said it was a map. Johnny said it looks like a river that has learned its route. Lydia said it looks like handwriting when a person is tired and still wants to be understood.

The town did what towns do. It folded me into the part of itself that keeps all the names and their weights. It gossiped cruelty once or twice in a tone it thought was kind, then stopped because the gossipers looked small next to the work of hands. The ferrymen kept on. New arrivals. Old decisions. Bella added to the freezer. She found a lock that made her feel better. It will not keep out sorrow. It will keep out the curious.

On the morning they walked Ella Street to the corner where the mailboxes lean and watched the sky decide its color, the male cardinal sang the three then two, and Johnny answered without looking around to see if anyone heard. He stood at the window. He whistled what his mouth could manage. The bird gave him the rest. They built a tune that did not ask to be written down. It was not an anthem. It was not a hymn. It was the sound two living things make when they stand on either side of glass and agree to meet in the middle.

This is the part I like to imagine because imagining is a right I kept. The house holds the echo of a whistle that does not belong to ferrymen. It belongs to a red bird on a fence post with a string tied around it and a man who knows the road to a kitchen he does not own and keeps walking it even after the world says he does not have to. The tune is small. It fits in the mouth. It is not catchy. It fades when the kettle boils and returns when the yard goes quiet. It says nothing more complicated than, here. It says nothing more complicated than, I hear you.

They say the male keeps coming. He does not bring another to the post. Not yet. He tests the branches and the wires and the roofline where ice used to live. He whistles. The two then three. The cheer. The long sliding note that he invented for himself the morning he met Johnny's sound. He does not sing it every day. He does not owe anyone consistency. He owes himself the work that keeps wings moving, and he does it without making a law of it.

And Johnny keeps the window closed. He is not making a bargain with anything that knocks. He is making a practice with something that perches. He whistles when he can. He goes silent when the song belongs to the air and his mouth cannot add to it. He fills the feeder and does not watch to see who comes. He knows who will come when it matters.

Bella writes all of this down. Not in the blue book. That is for ferrymen and the acts we choose or refuse. She keeps a new notebook in her freezer with a small label on the spine in her tidy hand.

Songs.

She will not show it to anyone who does not ask three times. She will leave it to no one in particular when she dies, because that is how you keep a tune from becoming a doctrine. It will live in a drawer until someone needs paper and finds it, and then the pages will come loose and one will end up under a magnet on a refrigerator. It will hold a line that says, he whistled, and the bird answered, and no one will know exactly when or where, and that is as it should be.

The ferrymen still come when they come. People still decide what to give. Names still leave mouths like breath in cold air. Quiet still enters houses and stays like a cat that chose you. A pair on a fence can break and leave the line half full. A man and a bird can choose a time of day and a tune and meet there without giving anything away. The kettle still clicks when it cools. Doors still open and close, even when no one is in the doorway. The yard still holds its shape, with a little red string to show where a branch was once the right kind of branch.

On some nights, if you walk the block and stop by the side yard of the kitchen with the window that learned when to open and when to stay shut, you can hear a small whistle ride the dark. You can hear another answer. You can know, without needing to see, that the male stands at his spot and the man stands at his, and between them there is a tune that keeps both from breaking, for a while, in a world that likes to ask for more than we can give.

They do not pretend the song changes what happened. It does not fill the space on the fence. It does not make spring come quicker. It gives a body a task that is not a bargain. It moves breath through a chest that needs to remember how to breathe. It tells the mind that has learned to make rooms with few windows that sound can cross where hands cannot. It counts a day. It ends when both feel finished. It begins again when one of them cannot help but lift his head and try.

Spring slid into a hot, slow summer. The male kept the post. He learned the habits of the light. He arrived before the sun cleared the trees, then again when the roof threw a thin shade. He whistled three then two, the little shape he and Ellis had made between glass and air. Some days he added the cheer. Some days he stayed quiet and let the yard speak for him.

Johnny held up his end. He stood at the window with his fingers at his lips and sent the notes out. He kept his eyes on the bird, not on his own reflection. He filled the feeder and swept the porch and learned the sound of the kettle all over again. He did the chores a body does to keep from turning into a room with the chairs stacked. He slept in the chair anyway some nights. He said it helped his back. Bella believed him in part. She also knew what the chair means when it becomes a habit.

By August the red string around the fence post had lost some color and settled into the grain. Lydia wrapped fresh twine over the old, a quiet doubling. She said the boy would have liked that. He liked repairs. She did not say the bird would notice. Birds notice in their own way.

The ferrymen kept to their own schedules, which is to say they came when they wanted to and never when asked. The town managed. People opened and refused and went on with hands that remembered how to fold laundry even when their minds felt like a deck with cards missing. Bella kept the blue notebook near and the songs notebook in the freezer with a neat label. She added a line now and then. He whistled at dusk. The bird answered from the post. A tune with three notes, then two.

Then one morning in late September, he did not come.

Johnny waited. He whistled once, then twice, then did not try to fill the silence. He stood by the sink with his hands on the edge and felt the house lean in. He checked the arbor and the wire and the apple branch. He scanned the roofline where heat shiver makes the world look like a veil. He looked beyond what he could see. Nothing red moved.

Nothing red moved the next day either. Or the day after. A single feather showed up near the downspout, not fresh, not a sign. A hawk shadow cut the yard at noon. A cat slept under the grill. The string stayed bright because Lydia had made it so. The post looked naked anyway.

Bella came at noon with bread and oranges. She stood at the window with him and took off her glasses to wipe them, though they were not dirty. She said, "he may be with a new flock." She said, "birds go. They do not owe us return." He nodded as if to agree. He did not argue with biology. He kept watching the post because that is where the song had lived.

The days stacked. The morning stayed the same, then did not. The whistle began to sound like something a person does to keep breath moving, not a call. Johnny tried to move the sound to evening. He stood in the last light and sent the three then two into the yard as if the tune itself could call a shape back into a place. Night answered with insects and a train far off.

Pain found its way to his joints and stayed. The winter salt work had got into his knees years ago and never left. The chair became more than a habit. The pills came from a bottle with his name on it. The bottle came from a drawer. The drawer filled, emptied, filled. Friends offered soup. He took it. He pretended it was enough. Some nights he chased the ache with whatever sat cold in the door of the fridge. He said it helped him sleep. He did not say anything about the mornings it did not.

Bella asked him straight, once. "Are you safe?"

He said, "I am fine." He said it with a voice that lives between truth and a wish. She did not press. She stayed longer than she had planned. She washed two cups and dried them. She put the dish towel on its hook because small order helps, even if it helps no one for long.

On the last Sunday of October, the sky carried that high bright light that makes everything look honest. Johnny stood at the window as he always did. He whistled the tune twice. He listened. Air. He put his palm on the glass and felt the cool. He looked past the post at the far fence and the road beyond that. He tried a different tune, something he had heard long ago on a radio while driving the salt route. It came out wrong. He smiled at himself. He shook his head. He sent the small three then two one more time and let it end where it ended.

That evening he sat in the chair with the TV talking to itself and the lamp left on. He took his pills. "More than he meant to," is what Bella would say later, because she needed to say something. He drank and did not count. He wanted quiet and sleep and the way a body can float for a while when the mind is heavy. He did not want to die that night. He wanted to lie down inside the noise and turn it down without opening any window at all.

He did not wake.

Bella found him in the morning when he did not answer the knock. She had a key for times like this. She called out his name in the hall the way a person calls into a cave to learn if it opens. The chair held him. The TV had turned to a blue screen without asking anyone. The kettle sat on the stove as if it had been waiting for the click. She put her hand on his shoulder, then drew it back, then put it there again because that is what you do when the world will not decide what it is. She called. She did what people do. She watched the room do its part, which is nothing. Later, someone wrote the word "overdose" on a line. Later, someone else wrote accidental and meant it.

There were no ferrymen at the window. No tapping. The work of the red birds had never been about this. This belonged to a different ledger. It came from a human drawer and a human night and the way a person can ask their body to be quiet and ask a little too hard.

Lydia arrived with a coat over pajamas and stood in the doorway and did not cross the threshold until Bella held out a hand. Johnny's hat hung on the peg like a period at the end of a sentence. The room smelled like what rooms smell like when someone sleeps and does not wake. Notations. Not evidence.

By afternoon, the house had more people than it should and all the wrong ones and all the right ones. A deputy with soft eyes. A woman with calm shoes who had been to my house before and knew how to stand back. A neighbor with a loaf wrapped in a towel. The town does this. It gathers, then it leaves, then it returns with something in a dish.

Bella cleaned the cup from the sink because she could. Lydia put the bread on a plate. Someone turned off the TV. Someone else turned it back on to know there was still noise in the world. The red string out back tugged a little in the breeze. The post held.

Johnny's name went into the blue notebook where it did not exactly belong. Bella argued with herself, then wrote it anyway. She added a line to the songs book too. Bird absent for weeks. Man whistled the tune alone. House answered with quiet.

At dusk, Bella went to the window. She put two fingers to her lips and tried the three then two. It came out thin. That was fine. Not every sound must be strong to count. The post stayed empty. The yard held its breath for her and then breathed like a yard again.

She tied a short length of red string beside the old. Not as a shrine. As a marker that says here, someone waited, and here, someone sang. She left the window shut. She stood in the kitchen as the kettle clicked once, then again, a small machine doing the work it had always done. She poured water into a cold sink and listened to how it sounded in this new quiet.

The next morning, the mail came and the news spread in the way news spreads in places like this. At the diner, a waitress turned a cup upside down and left it that way. On the salt route, a truck rode slower by the corner with the leaning mailboxes. On the church steps, someone crossed herself and did not know why since it was not her language. Mrs. Darrow touched both her mismatched chairs and said two names under her breath, alternating. Lydia poured coffee and spoke three names into it before she drank. One for the boy. One for me. One for Ellis. She did not look for the right order. The cup did not ask.

The male cardinal did not come back. Not that day. Not the week after. Not when November stuttered and found its cold again. There were other birds. Sparrows at the edge of the shrubs. A wren that scolded without needing a reason. A hawk far up, a double brushstroke when the light hit right. The post remained. The red string held a darker line of weather where the older layer had been.

On a clear morning in early winter, Bella opened the freezer and took out the songs notebook. She turned to the back page and wrote, *last entry. Bird gone. Man gone. Tune remains in the mouth.* She closed the book and put it back among the cold things. She leaned on the counter and put her head down on her arms and stayed there until the kettle clicked.

Sometimes, now, when evening draws its thin line across the yard, you can hear a whistle cut the air near the kitchen window, not loud, not even skillful. Someone walking past, maybe. Someone who knew the man. Three notes, then two. A small practice, not a bargain. The post takes it. The string, faded and doubled, takes it. The house takes it. The air holds it for a second longer than you expect and then gives it back to the quiet that knows how to carry weight without dropping it.

Red Couriers

The winter the cardinals started tapping again, the town opened its curtains instead of closing them.

We had learned one thing from the ferrymen.

Loss wants dark.

Love wants light.

The first knocks ask for names.

The second kind does not ask for anything you can write down.

You learn to tell the weight by the seam it presses in your breath.

On a Thursday that froze the steps into glass, I heard three taps on my kitchen window. Not the hard knuckle of the ferrymen. Softer. Like a fingernail on a teacup. The sound made the kettle hesitate, then gather itself again.

A male cardinal sat on the sill. Red as a wound and a ribbon both. He cocked his head. His crest lifted once. He held a sprig in his beak, thin and brown, with a twist of red thread around it. He did not enter. He did not leave. He waited as if time were a blanket he could sit on until I remembered where I kept the word yes.

I kept my hands on the kettle because hands like work, especially when the room begins to tilt. Then I set the kettle down. Then I went to the window. The floor felt newly mapped; not dangerous, only unfamiliar.

"Not today," I said out of habit. It was the sentence that kept me upright the winter the ferrymen learned our street. You can live a month on a sentence if you smooth it with your thumb and keep it where your mouth can find it.

He tapped once more as if to say, it is not that kind of day. He did not flinch when a salt truck hissed past and the driver whistled two notes that tried and failed to answer him.

I could feel a heat on the glass where his body sat. It was a small heat. Enough to make a fog ring by the edge of his tail. The ring faded. He stayed. I raised my palm and did not touch, the way you hover your hand over a sleeping child, not to wake, only to know.

A knock came at my door. Not the window. A woman with snow in her hair stood there without a hat. She stamped once, not to be dramatic, only to be polite to my floor.

"Chester," she said. "I'm Bella Morgan. North Carolina State Office. Field Division Two. We met when the ferrymen came. I think your bird is not a ferryman."

"He brought a twig," I said. Talking calms the part of me that wants to flee an invitation.

"They bring tokens," she said. "These are couriers. We call them Bridgers in the old files. They arrive with pieces you can use."

"To do what?"

"To make a thing you thought you could not make again."

I noticed then how the light gathered around the sill, a pale halo, as if the cold itself wanted to see. The street outside hissed with salt and tires. Somewhere a neighbor's kettle clicked and steadied. The bird adjusted his grip and the red thread winked like a vein. The house leaned toward the glass, the way houses do when a threshold remembers its job.

"Do I speak first?" I asked.

"You can," Bella said. "Or you can listen and say the true thing after. Both work, if you mean it."

I breathed on the pane. The fog on my side met the faint warmth on his. Where they touched, a little clear circle formed, a keyhole with no key, only willingness. I thought of Talinda, how she used to test a skillet with two drops of water and wait for the right sound. The circle on the glass made the same kind of sense. The day said "ready" without raising its voice.

Bella stepped inside and did not take off her coat. She had a folder tucked under her arm the way people carry babies when they have not held many. She laid it on my table and did not open it. Her gloves stayed in her pocket. Her eyes took the room's temperature and seemed content to let it be.

"Before the ferrymen," she said, "there were stories of red couriers."

"Fewer."

"They were ignored because death is easier to count than love. North Carolina prefers numbers that do not argue."

"What do they ask for," I asked, nodding at the bird, grateful to have a question with a hinge I could see.

"Not payment," she said. "Anchor. Love slides if you don't weight it. They ask you to promise a small act before they drop what they bring."

"What kind of act?"

"Truth," she said. "To yourself or someone else. A confession you can live with. A kindness you owe. It varies. It should be measurable by the body, not just the mouth."

The male tapped again. He held the sprig up as if offering a pen. I unlatched the window before I could think. The cold hit my face. The bird did not fly inside. He leaned and set the sprig on the sill with the care of a person placing a glass on someone else's table. Then he stepped back, not like a servant, like a witness.

"What do I do with it?" I asked.

"Make a first thing," Bella said. "Anything that can hold a second. A frame, a bowl, a place on a shelf that was empty because you were certain nothing good would ever sit there again."

I pressed my palm to the glass near his feet and felt that small heat again. It went through the pane. Or I imagined it. Imagination is a tool. It built cathedrals and patched roofs and keeps widowers from mistaking numbness for safety.

I said the only confession I could stand to bring into speech. "I am afraid to love anything I can name."

"That will do," Bella said. "Start there. Do not embroider it. Lace comes later if it comes at all."

The bird flicked his crest. He sang two notes and a third that slid toward sweet. He lifted from the sill without fuss and went to the fence post where the ferrymen had once waited. He stood there and looked official and kind. It is possible for a creature to be both.

I thought of the nurse who took Talinda's pulse on her last good morning. "Steady", she had said, with a face that knew the word had a dozen meanings.

"Put the sprig where you do dishes," Bella said, watching my face instead of the bird. "Love returns best to the places hands already know. Sinks. Tables. Lamps switched on first thing. The workstations of a life."

I laid the sprig on the window ledge above the basin. The thread made a small question mark. The kettle popped and whispered. Outside, the cardinal leaned into a pale wind and did not yield. I felt my shoulders drop a fraction, a notch any carpenter would recognize. Fit. Not finish. Start, not story yet. My mouth found the shape of a quiet thank you and kept it behind my teeth so it would not scare anything away.

We had rules for the ferrymen.

Felt.

Psalms.

Closed latches.

The couriers changed our posture. People pulled chairs to their windows. They boiled extra water. They wrote letters and did not mail them. They made toasts to empty rooms. We are not a town that does parades for feelings, but we will line both sides of a kitchen counter if there is a chance something gentle might arrive.

Word moved like steam. Quick.

Quiet once it hit the cold.

There was a woman on Sycamore who opened for a courier on a Monday and by Thursday had made a quilt out of torn shirts from a marriage she thought was over. Her husband came home without knowing why, sat in the living room, and said the house felt like it had a new floor under it. When he saw the quilt, he cried twice, once at the colors and once at the stitching he recognized. He said her name in a register he had not used in years. Later he wiped his face with the sleeve he used to hide. Then he folded two shirts without being asked.

There was a boy who had stopped speaking. The courier brought him a marble he had lost under a radiator when he was six. He held it up to the light and said the word blue like a prayer. His father wrote the word on a card and taped it by the latch so the house would remember the temperature it had just learned.

There was a nurse who could not touch her own hand without flinching. A courier left a clover with four leaves in her pocket. She found it when she went to buy coffee and felt her fingers rest on her palm and not recoil. The love it opened did not rush to a person. It moved through her body like light finding its path in a room with new paint. She came to Nora's and ate without apologizing for being hungry.

"They bring love," Bella said. "Not romance. Though sometimes that too. They deliver the capacity to bind. The old files call it 'return'."

At the library, someone found an old date stamp in a drawer and began stamping the word "KEPT" on index cards left by the windows. At the grocery, the clerk started setting aside bruised fruit in a bowl labeled "Practice". People took one piece and wrote a name on the chalkboard and called it "anchoring". The choir director who had lost his pitch last winter hummed along with the heater and found the key again. We started to greet each other with questions that had answers.

"Anchored yet?"

"Not yet. Soon." I promised the chair. I promised the call.

"Make me ask you tomorrow." We learned how to mean the asking.

The couriers came and went as if on their own clock, a schedule not made for us but willing to include us. Red on posts, brown in hedges, a flash at the wire, a tap like a teaspoon, tokens placed where the eye would find them and the hand would not be afraid. I made a habit of rinsing the sill with a warm cloth at dusk the way Talinda used to rinse the sink after the last cup, not because it needed it, because care prefers to be practiced when no one is taking notes.

Bella brought the folder the next day. She opened it and showed me pages thin with age. A parish letter from 1963 about red couriers in years of famine, a doctor's note from a clinic with a heater that worked half the time, a typed page titled "Affinities and Returns". There were no numbers. Only hand names, dates, the weather, and the quiet phrase delivered and anchored. In the margin of one page a small coffee ring made the O in love look like a moon.

"Anchored," I said. "What is that?"

"The act that keeps the gift from dissolving."

"How do you anchor?"

"By doing the thing you promised you would do."

"To who?"

"To anyone to whom you have owed it long enough to be embarrassed," she said. "Shame is a poor ruler, but it can be a good compass if you hold it lightly."

I thought of two names I had not spoken to in months. One belonged to a friend I had left for dead out of laziness. One belonged to a version of myself I pretended had never lived. I could feel Talinda's silence at my shoulder, not accusing, waiting to see if I wanted to be the man she saw on our better days.

"Begin small," Bella said, reading my face the way good neighbors read sky.

The male courier returned with a new token. A button. Mother of pearl. He held it between his bill and set it on the sill with a sound like rain starting on a pan. I touched the glass with two fingers. I said, "I will apologize to the friend." It felt like a draft that would stop when the door found its frame.

"Good," Bella said. "Do it before the kettle clicks. Heat helps truth loosen without tearing."

I called. The friend answered. We are not good at fine words here. We use bowls instead. I said, "I am sorry." She said, "I know," and laughed once, short and kind, and described a dream in which I had carried her from a very small fire. We made tea in our separate kitchens. We drank as if we had agreed to share a cup through the wall. After we hung up, I sat in the chair Talinda always claimed when she wanted to see the sky and said my own name out loud to check if it still fit.

The button went into the blue notebook on a page labeled "Tokens". We began a second notebook. "Songs." Bella kept it in my freezer, wrapped tight, with a tidy label. Freezers are for things you cannot afford to spoil. The State could pry a cabinet open. It would not search among peas. I slid the sprig under the string of an empty frame that had waited a year to hold anything but dust.

"Look," Bella said, turning one of the old pages so I could see the penciled margin. Someone long gone had written, *Anchor = weight you can lift*. "They knew," she said. "It's not punishment. It's ballast. Enough to keep the boat from smacking itself silly."

She told me a case from the file. 1902. A mill town in the mountains of North Carolina, hard winter. Red birds tapped at panes that had been stuffed with newspaper. A woman was given a single straight pin and told herself she'd mend one thing a day until the thaw. She mended cuffs, then flags, then a child's hat. By spring the town had a line of coats on a cord and a habit of leaving one empty hook at every door. *Delivered and anchored,* the priest had written. Weather, cruel. People, steady. I copied the sentence on an index card and taped it near the latch so my hands would have something honest to read.

People think love is a flood. The couriers showed us it behaves more like water in a kettle. It heats quiet. It clicks when it is ready. You pour it where you thought nothing could grow and wait. If you keep staring at it, it makes a fool of you. If you turn away to set a bowl, it arrives.

The town did what towns do with a strange mercy. It made forms without numbers.

"Chester, have you anchored?"

"Timmy, have you apologized?"

"Mrs. Darrow, who are you confessing to this week?"

We sounded like a club and a choir both, out of tune but loud. The new habit made our old arguments seem bored with themselves.

Nora from the church basement cooked three new soups. One for people who needed to say a thing. One for people who needed to hear it. One for people who had to keep quiet longer than was fair. She put the recipes on cards with grease at the corners and a line at the bottom that read, *bell after bowls.*

The State Office stayed two steps behind. It called a meeting. Bella brought pamphlets with diagrams she did not like and did not hand out. *Consent and Anchoring. Couriers and You.* She put them under a plant and hoped the plant would drink the ink. Later she used one to catch a drip from a slow pipe. "Government paper finally doing some good," she said, and we laughed because we needed to.

"Do they ever harm?" I asked in the corner where a radiator hissed.

"They can flood a person who will not anchor," she said. "Love without weight makes you frantic. You open all your windows and the house counts as empty. Then you blame the wind for your choice."

"Has that happened here?"

"Not yet," she said. "We learned to keep each other in rooms. We built small dams you can step over."

Kopek's placed a saucer by the big window and wrote on a chalkboard, *Take one truth, leave one chair.* The barber stopped turning the radio up when somebody cried. He handed them a towel instead, slow, neat, the way he always folded the back of a collar. Kids chalked the two note call on the sidewalk in little dashes, and some afternoons you could walk the whole block by stepping from note to note and never touching bare concrete. When a door stayed too open for too long, somebody stood in it and asked, "Anchor first, neighbor," with a grin that said we were protecting our windows, not policing hearts. That line saved three friendships and one porch from turning into a sermon.

At dusk the kettles clicked in half the kitchens on Oak at the same time, an unplanned carillon. The birds answered from the wires, two notes, then a third that slid toward sweet. We learned not to clap. You do not applaud heat. You pour it. I set two bowls every night for a month, one for me and one for a name, and ate both slowly. The second bowl stayed warm longer than made sense. I did not investigate.

The female courier came on a Sunday. Brown, warm, crest like a pen. She tapped once. She did not bring a twig. She brought a piece of paper curled tight as if it had been in a pocket for years. She set it down and looked at me. She did not look through me. Love is a looking at. Death is a looking past. The ferrymen had looked past. This one set her gaze like a chair I was invited to sit in.

I placed my palm on the glass. "What anchor?" I asked the room, not the bird. My voice had that dry edge it gets when a word you have put off returns and refuses to wait on the porch.

"Tell yourself the truth," Bella said behind me. She has a talent for arriving when sentences careen. She leaned on the doorframe like a comma that keeps two parts from colliding.

"I am afraid to love anything I can name," I said again. It was true and not enough. The room did not lighten. It steadied.

"And?" she asked.

"And I have loved in a way that made smaller loves starve." Saying it loosened a knot behind my right shoulder that grief had claimed as its desk.

"Better," she said. "Say where you learned it."

"In the long winter of Talinda's last year," I answered. "I fed the wrong fires because I was afraid the right one would go out."

I opened the window an inch. The paper slid in on a small gust. The female lifted and went to the fence post where a length of red twine had survived winter. She stood on it and watched, the way a good teacher watches you copy your own work without cheating.

The paper contained a line in my own hand from a year I had not dared to reread. I had written to my wife, Talinda, when she was sick. I had put the letter in a drawer and lost the drawer in a move and told myself the letter was for a person who would not see it anyway. The line said, *I will carry your winter as long as I can and then I will ask for help.*

It is hard to love the person who asked for help in your name. It is harder to love the person who did not. I was both men in one body.

I called Nora. I asked if she needed a hand at the dinner. She did. Love is a soup line with a bad ladle and two good shoulders. After the call, I sat with the paper and traced the groove of my own writing with a finger as if it were a seam that could be pressed open. The female watched from the post. I thought of the last winter in that other kitchen, the one with her cough and the way we rationed our words like tea. I said Talinda's name once, and the room did not break. The paper smelled faintly of oranges and dust. I slid it into a frame of thread and sprig and button and called the frame nothing at all. A place for my eye to land when the day tilted. Love, returned, needs a landing more than it needs applause.

Timmy, the new salt truck driver, tied a red cloth to his mailbox and asked the couriers for a delivery. They did not come. He sang to the truck the way Johnnt always had, with the windows down in cold. The couriers do not answer wishes. They answer readiness. Timmy took the cloth down after a week and put a bell on the inside knob where only his hand would ring it. That counted as listening.

One came when he stopped asking. It left a bolt with a thread that fit a door on his truck that rattled for years. He fixed the door and then drove to a house he had been avoiding. He put his hand on the bell and kept it there until someone answered. It was his daughter. She wore her hair in a way that looked like work. They said each other's names. They set soup on a table. They did not ask for the past to make a speech.

They anchored.

Later, he brought the bolt to Nora's and set it in the dish of tokens like a man laying down a coin he intended to spend again.

Mia at the Pine Street shop came in with a brown bag and put a book on the workbench.

Poems.

She said a courier had left it on her stoop with a button half sewn into the spine. The button matched a missing one on a coat that had hung in her shop since fall. She sewed the button on and called the number pinned inside. The owner cried in three languages and came the next morning with coffee. They did not talk about the winter. They talked about the hem and the weather and whether the cedar would split straight if you asked it nicely.

Lydia from the blue house by the creek sat with a cup and said her boy's name out loud into steam. The couriers did not take it. They never take. They only bring the capacity to say and hear. She folded a paper crane and left it on her sill. A male landed beside it and flicked his crest and the room warmed. She kneaded dough and did not check the clock. The loaf rose when it was ready and not a minute sooner.

Later that week Timmy's daughter brought him a small tin whistle, the kind from parades. He put it on his dash and did not blow it until he had fixed three more rattles he had promised himself he would ignore. When he did, the note came out ragged and then right. He grinned at the windshield, a man with a tune in his pocket again. Mia, closing shop, found a straight pin in her apron she did not remember putting there. She mended the cuff of her own sleeve, then the hem on the coat of a woman who always said no when asked if she needed anything. Lydia braided two loaves and burned one and smiled through it. The unburned one fed three people who arrived without warning and left a jar ring on her counter in return. These were small economies. They changed the weather inside our houses.

"There are kinds of couriers," Bella said. "Not official, no badges. You can tell by the tokens." She spoke like a person who had tried to diagram a river and finally accepted the value of a list.

The Name Returners bring a letter you wrote yourself and could not face, or a photograph that seemed to vanish when you needed it most, or a voice recording that plays once and never again. They do not give back the dead. They give back the name's place in your mouth and do not charge you for saying it. They make room around the syllables so they stop bruising your teeth.

The Heat Bearers bring little things that make rooms give back heat. A twig that smells like a summer you loved. A coin that warm hands held. A strip of fabric from a dress you danced in and forgot. They do not warm the whole house. They make the stove answer when you ask politely.

The Sight Lenders bring a way of seeing small acts as love. A cup set out. A door oiled. A pencil sharpened without comment. They deliver a lens. You learn to keep it clean. If you press it too hard to your eye, it fogs and you blame the lens. If you hold it lightly, the day sharpens without hurting.

"And then," she said.

"There is a fourth," I said, smiling at her, because by then I had learned to hear the hinge in her voice.

"One that comes at dusk," she said. "It brings a test."

"What test?"

"Whether you can keep your own borders when love stands very near. Whether you can tell the difference between invitation and flood."

"There's maybe a fifth," Bella added, almost to herself. "They don't bring tokens. They bring timing. They make two people reach for the latch at once."

"What do we call them?"

"Keepers of the Latch," she said, and shrugged. "I haven't seen one. I've only seen the result. Two apologies colliding in a doorway. A silence that lets one person speak without losing the other. A chair pulled closer at the exact second before a knee gives out."

We started to jot the categories on a card by the sink like a cook might list substitutions.

No rosemary, use thyme.

No bravery, use habit.

No eloquence, use a bowl.

The dusk kind tested us most. We printed the rule below it in red pencil. *Anchor first. Window after.* The card yellowed fast from steam. We made more. I added, ask Talinda for her counsel, which meant say her name before I touched a latch.

The dusk courier came on a day that smelled like thaw. He sat on the sill and did not tap. He watched me with that steady patience the ferrymen used, but the weight was different. The ferrymen taught you how to live with absence. The dusk courier asked if you were sure you wanted presence. Both questions were honest. Only one asked you to wash your cup after.

He carried nothing I could see. He brought a tilt in the room. Air leaned toward the window as if a door had opened elsewhere in the house. The kettle, faithful as a dog, kept to its work.

"What anchor?" I asked. My voice found its map quicker than my feet.

Bella did not answer. She had stepped into the hall to make coffee and went quiet in the way that means a person trusts you to know the right sentence. The silence had the feel of an open palm. Not pushing.

Waiting.

I spoke to the glass. "I will not make love a law." It felt like a map unfurling. I added, "I will not open every window and call it 'kindness'. I will choose a room and clean it." The last line belonged to Talinda. She used to say it when grief tried to make us run laps.

I lifted the latch a finger's width. The courier held still. My heart lifted hard in my chest and then settled. The bird sang a phrase I had not heard, three notes that rose and then descended as if someone had walked up a hill and sat down to watch the town catch its breath. The sound touched the old bruise and did not press.

Love arrived like heat. Not a flood. A kettle click. I felt my hands soften against the sink and my shoulders drop. The room did not change color. My mouth did. Words that had rusted at the edges rubbed clean. I could say "please" again without it scraping.

I did not think of a new person. I thought of the old ones and felt the ache shift from a fist to a palm. It held. It did not crush. The feeling had weight. I could carry it down the hall without dropping it on the corner where the rug curls.

When I closed the latch again, nothing was taken from me. A quiet stayed. The dusk courier hopped to the post, cocked his head, and gave the simple two note, as if to say, "practice that". I wrote my anchor on an index card and stuck it by the latch where my hand would find it tomorrow. Bella returned with two mugs and did not ask what had happened, the best kind of witness. We drank. Outside, ice softened on the fence, then found its edge again when the sun slipped. The house kept its shape.

So did I.

Later, I whistled the three notes alone in the hallway and did not feel foolish.

We had a meeting in the library basement again. The carpet still smelled like it needed sun. The chairs were the same. The cookies looked right and tasted like someone's best try. People spoke in turns. They did not discuss doctrine. They told what had happened and what they had promised and whether they had kept it. The bell on the table made a small move when someone told the truth. No one pretended it was a miracle. We called it a draft.

A woman in a neat coat said a courier had brought her a pin shaped like a crescent moon. She wore it to a job she hated and said to her boss, "I cannot be the version of me you think I am". He said the company did not recognize versions. She said "thank you" and left. Love does not always keep you where you are. It can usher you to the door and hand you your coat. She brought the pin to the dish at Nora's and took a jar ring in trade. The sound her keys made later told me the day had approved.

A young person with a ring through their brow said a courier had left three paper hearts on their stoop. They gave them to three neighbors who had never spoken to each other. Those neighbors brought soup when the pipes burst, unasked. The hearts got wet on the counter and no one minded. Paper can hold kindness even when it curls.

A man with sleeves cut off from a sweater said a courier delivered a yo-yo, a tin one from a childhood he had tried to disown. He spun it in his kitchen and his wife laughed like the person she had been when they were greedy and tired and in love without paperwork. They put the yo-yo on a shelf next to three bills and a photograph that should have been thrown away but still did work. He said he had apologized for the winter he spent in the garage pretending the engine needed him more than his family. He called the apology "his ballast."

Bella sat and did not speak while we spoke.

She does not lead.

She witnesses.

She writes later, in tidy hand, in the blue notebook, under headings that matter only to her.

"Delivered and anchored."

"Weather."

"Names spoken without harm."

"Misuse corrected."

"Quiet held."

"Kettle count at dusk."

Mrs. Darrow raised a hand and said she had set two mismatched chairs at one table and invited a woman she had disliked for thirty years to sit in the better one. They ate soup and said nothing mean. She called that "an anchor". A boy from the back said he had sharpened three pencils for someone who never remembered to bring one and had not told the teacher it was him. The room murmured, approval as instruction. At the end, we stacked the chairs and left the carpet to its stubborn smell. Someone had taped an index card to the basement door. *Anchor first*, it said in a child's print. *Window after.* We touched it as we passed, the way people touch stones in older places and do not call it "superstition." Outside, the air held a tune under its tongue. We walked home and let it follow at a respectful distance.

The State did not know what to do with love. It sent paper where we had placed bowls. It issued a flyer that told people to check with their physicians before accepting a token. It suggested consulting a counselor to avoid spikes of affective intensity. It reminded us that the State was not responsible for outcomes. Bella put the flyers in a drawer and labeled it, "Panics." She kept the blue notebook under the peas. She said peas hold their shape in an argument and led me back to the sink to practice the two notes until the kettle clicked.

We heard there might be a hotline. There was talk of a registry. A man in a tie asked if couriers could be scheduled by district. Bella said "the birds did not read memos". He wrote that down as if it might help. She smiled at him until he stopped. He tried again with a grid that carved our blocks into squares. Love does not like being folded to fit a chart. He left with one of Nora's recipes in his pocket and the smell of onions on his cuffs.

"We are not making a program," she said. "We are making a practice."

"Programs have money," I said. My voice had the old grit that comes when a bill sits under a magnet longer than is kind.

"Practice has bowls and a kettle," she said. "We will be fine."

"Fine" is a word we forgive in winter. It means not collapsing. It also means we will try again tomorrow with the same pot and the same spoon. The best practices in town were built from repetition that did not demand applause: A chair pulled close; A towel folded neat; A name set gently on a plate and returned with a clean edge.

We did have to make rules. The most important was simple. Do not open for a courier if you are planning to make a person into a door. Say your anchor first. Promise the thing, then receive. We wrote it on index cards and taped them near latches. We said it aloud in the library basement until the sentence lost its vanity and kept its bones.

We learned to ask each other to anchor.

"What did you promise, Chester?" Mrs. Darrow would say at the mailboxes.

"Who do you owe?" Timmy would ask from the truck.

It sounded nosy.

It was care.

We backed the questions with quiet. Ten seconds after the question, no advice. A nod and a bell if the person named something true. The nod traveled down Oak Street and took up residence in our wrists. We could feel when someone had kept a promise even before they told us what it was.

Nora posted a list behind the soup line. *Anchors we accept. Truth. Apology. Labor. Rest. Anchors we refuse. Grand gestures that cost someone else. Speeches that hide an appetite.* We signed our names under the first list. We left the second blank. Empty lines can instruct. The empty lines kept us from inventing fancy sins to excuse our plain ones.

The flyers arrived again a week later with new language. The State suggested a cooling period after tokens. It recommended a signature in duplicate for any promise made in the presence of a bird. We laughed and put the papers under the table legs that rocked. Useful at last. The table steadied. So did we. A man at the end of the line pointed at the steadied table and said, "Government finally holding something up." Nobody argued. We passed him a bowl.

One afternoon Bella took me to the office where the State stored its forms in tidy towers. She handed in a report on plain paper with four lines. "Delivered. Anchored. Weather. Names spoken without harm." The clerk asked for attachments. Bella pointed at me and said, "witness." The clerk asked for data. Bella said, "hot kettles at dusk," and placed a small jar of steam on the counter by taking a lid off a thermos at the right time. The clerk's glasses fogged. He removed them, laughed once, and stamped our sheet with "Received." It felt like a permission no one owned.

The pair behind my kitchen took a post near the apple tree. He came first most days. She followed in a low arc. They traded seeds the way all cardinals do when they believe the day belongs to them. The ferrymen had used the post for dispatches. The couriers used it for courtship. The same place can hold different kinds of work without breaking. I learned to wash the sill like a table that expects company.

I added a shallow dish for water with a heater bought used. It kept a ring from freezing at noon. The birds learned the timing. They drank with beaks lifted between sips like a blessing. When wind pressed, they turned their backs to it and trusted the hedge. They knew where to put their weight and when to keep it light. I watched and practiced the same in my kitchen, shoulders lined with the cabinet's edge, feet planted, voice soft.

I made a thing from the tokens. The sprig. The button. The paper with my own line returned to me. I wound the thread the birds had carried around a small frame and tied the sprig at the edge. I sewed the button to the corner and slid the paper behind the string. It looked like a child's project and a shrine both. I did not call it either. I called it, "place to look when the room goes grey." I kept it near the lamp Talinda liked to click on with her knuckle. The shade threw a small circle on the wall that held where the day had tried to slip.

I set the frame where the light lands first in the morning. I touched the glass beside it when I faltered. Not to warm it. To remind my palm it could hold instead of brace. The habit changed my shoulders before it changed my words. That was enough. When a sentence tried to run for the door, my hand found the glass and stayed. The sentence learned to be a neighbor instead of a thief.

I kept the window closed when I needed to. The couriers do not sulk. They perch and sing what they brought and leave it in the air like a word you can remember later if you practice. Some days I wrote the song down in the notebook and put it back in the freezer. Some days I hummed it once and let it go. There is a grace in letting a tune fade when it wants to fade.

On three afternoons the pair ignored the feeder entirely and fed each other from the ground. Beak to beak, small offer, small acceptance. That taught more than any pamphlet. The town learned to watch and then make one exchange of our own that day. A ride given. A bowl returned. A door oiled without note. We wrote those verbs on cards and propped them by latches like recipes. We cooked them until they tasted like us.

One evening, I stood at the sink and said Talinda's name twice, waiting to see if the room would tilt into grief. It did not. It tilted into work. The frame on the ledge caught the corner of my eye and gave me back my breath. I mended a shirt after I dried the last bowl. The stitch was not straight. The shirt forgave me. The day had room for my trying.

Bella had her own delivery. She did not tell me in a speech. She arrived one Sunday with a bag of oranges and a silence I recognized. She set the bag down. She opened the freezer and took out the blue notebook and set it on the table and put her hands on either side of it as if she were keeping it from sliding. When a person braces a book, they are bracing themselves. I took out the knife we use on bread and placed it far from the edge where hands fumble.

"A courier left a note," she said. "Not to me. To my mother. From my sister."

She said sister the way a person says water when a glass is near. She did not cry. She made the small movement with her mouth that people make when they have cried often and do not want to tax a room again. I nodded, the good nod, the one that says you may rest here.

"What anchor?" I asked. It felt cruel and right. We had taught each other to put the ballast on the table before we poured.

"I told my mother the truth," she said. "That I have been doing this so I could stand at thresholds and not pick a room. That I have not chosen a life because the courier work lets me pretend the doorway is a home. I said I will pick a room."

"What room?"

"I do not know," she said, and laughed in a way that let me know the choosing had already begun. The laugh had the small wind of relief in it. She had been carrying a door on her back and had finally set it down.

The note had the shape of her sister's hand, Bella said. Not the exact letter shapes. The pressure. The pauses between words. It said nothing new. It said everything. It said, "I loved you from the shallow end and the deep and I did not know the difference while I was swimming." It said, "bring a towel." It said, "I am beyond towels," and it was not cruel. It did not bring her back. It brought a love that did not beg for a reply. It set two chairs in a room and left.

We cut the oranges. We ate them over the sink. Juice ran. We let it. Bella folded the note and put it between two pages in the songs book for one night only. In the morning she carried it to her mother. They read it aloud twice. Then they made the bed. Some tokens want chores. Some want chairs. This one wanted both. When they were done, Bella moved her mother's chair three inches closer to the window and left a bell within reach. She did not say a word about it. Her mother rang it once that evening for the sound and once the next morning for the meaning.

At dusk the female courier landed on the post and did not tap. She watched the kitchen settle. She flicked her crest once. That was enough. I took it as a benediction that does not bother with pomp. We stood at the sink and let the house breathe around us. The kettle clicked like a clock that tells useful time.

Love can tip. People opened too many windows and talked too long at the diner and told secrets to strangers as if they were asking for a key. The town pressed back. We made quiet hours. We set chairs closer so people could touch a shoulder and stop a sentence turning into a flood. We learned to protect the practice from our appetites.

A man stood on a box outside the hardware store and shouted that the couriers were a cult. Timmy asked if we could have a cult that shovels. The man did not laugh. We did. Then we put our shovels in his truck and he drove away slowly, less angry, because carrying a weight on purpose helps. He came back the next day and bought a bell without announcing it. The receipt lived in his wallet under a child's drawing.

There were mistakes. A courier delivered to a house where a woman had practiced harm. She used the tokens to decorate a wall and called the wall "Love." We took the tokens and returned them to the sill and asked the pair to choose better. They did. Love is not impressed by displays. It prefers a sink with dishes and a clean towel. The woman came to Nora's and sat with empty hands. She did not speak for three dinners. On the fourth, she folded two towels and placed them at the end of the line. That counted. We counted it twice in our hearts and once in the book.

We wrote a new card.

What love is not:

It is not an excuse.

It is not a stage.

It is not a demand dressed as a vow.

We set the card by the fence table and folded two spares into coat pockets. When a porch got loud, someone set the card on the rail and the noise softened. The card kept us honest when our mouths tried to sell what our hands had not made.

Bella went to the State and argued for nothing. No forms. No quotas. No punishments. She came back with a face that said she had fought a river with a plate. She set the plate down and ate lasagna. She took the blue notebook from the freezer and wrote in tidy hand. *Delivered. Anchored. Weather.* Names spoken without harm. She added a line.

Misuse corrected, tokens returned. She closed the book and slid it back under the peas with a motion that said a day can be saved by putting the right thing back where it belongs.

We tried a different kind of quiet later. A circle at Nora's with no talking for ten minutes. The kettles clicked. The room breathed. The dusk courier sat on the sill and blinked once. People cried without needing an audience. When the bell rang, we left bowls in a neat stack and did not wash them until morning. Love can wait for soap. The stack said we trusted our future selves to do what was needed without a speech to make it holy.

Spring loosened the ground. The serviceberry by the back fence woke and budded. The pair sang the dawn song with more notes than usual, as if they had found a new angle on joy. The notes carried to the alley and into three kitchens at once. The town woke without an alarm.

I found a new angle myself. I opened to a courier and promised to say my own name in the morning. It felt vain and wrong and then right. I said, "Chester," and listened. The kitchen answered with the sound of the kettle and the click of the bulb in the lamp and my feet on the tile. The name sat up straight and looked around. It seemed to like the room. It looked less like a sentence and more like a chair.

Lydia began to write the names of strangers on slips of paper and put them under magnets on her refrigerator. She said their names over bread dough and made loaves that tasted like people doing their best. She sold some. She gave more away. She said it kept the boy near to put new names in his company. She told me grief will tolerate company if you give it good bread.

Timmy drove and sang and stopped once to fix a hinge on a gate that was not his and the woman who lived there came out and cried because the gate had stuck for a decade and she had used the stuckness to avoid seeing the neighbor who watered her flowers when she was out of town because she did not know how to say "thanks." She said "thanks." He said, "I wanted to whistle," and pushed the gate twice to show it could. He left without taking coffee because leaving clean is its own gift.

The dusk courier came once and I did not open. I kept my anchor anyway. I said, "I will not waste the good on people who use it as rope." It felt like a shield I could carry without hurting anyone. The bird blinked once as if to approve, then flew to the post where the pair traded a seed and a nod. I took the hint and saved my heat for those who would not hold it against me.

I added one more small anchor to my card. I will mend one thing a week. I started with a torn pocket. I moved to the loose rung on a chair. I tightened a hinge on a door that groaned. The work kept grief from turning to smoke. It gave it weight and a place. When the pair traded a seed on the post, I nodded to no one and to them both. We were learning the same lesson at different scales.

Give.

Take.

Guard.

Rest.

Talinda would have approved. She liked any plan that made hands honest and rooms calmer by nightfall.

There is an end here, and there is not. The couriers do not go. They rest in summer. They return when mornings turn hard. They deliver little things that heavy days cannot crush. A button. A twig. A line in your own hand. They do not want your sorrow. They want your promise. If you keep that, they keep coming. If you do not, they wait without pouting.

We did not become a town without grief. We became a town with bowls and chairs and windows that open for the right knocks. The ferrymen still visit sometimes. We do not hiss at them. Some people need a quiet they cannot make alone. We witness. We hold doors while they open the window and say a word and keep living with a blank that no one should judge. The ferrymen bring a winter that must be named. The couriers bring a spring that must be tended. We learned to hold both seasons without lying.

Most days now, the post behind my kitchen holds a pair of birds doing the work the world gave them. He lands. She follows. He feeds. She accepts. They both watch for hawk shadows. They both drink when the ring thaws. They sing a song that is not for us, and we borrow it anyway. We keep a notebook in the freezer labeled "Songs". We write down the day and the weather and the line we needed to hear. We do not show it to anyone who has not asked three times. The third ask matters. It scatters the showmanship before it can grow legs.

In the evening, I stand at the sink and press my palm to the glass. The heat on the other side is more habit than weather. The house leans the way houses do when someone is home. The kettle clicks. The threshold bell moves once. The two on the post make small sounds that do not have to be metaphors.

They are birds.

They are not messengers.

They are messengers.

They carry what they carry. They bring the shape of love back to a mouth that thought it had lost its words. I whistle the three note into the drain to see if the house remembers. It does.

When a courier taps, I listen. If I open, I anchor. If I do not, I still say the names I have kept. I say my own. I say Bella's in the morning sometimes, into coffee, because friends belong with first heat. I say Lydia's when the dough rises. I say Timmy's when the truck rounds the corner and the song hangs in air. I say Mrs. Darrow's when I see two mismatched chairs facing one table. I do not say the dead as bargains. I say them as company. Talinda sits beside the lamp when I say her name and makes no demands. That is the mercy of practice.

The couriers do not require thanks. I say it anyway: to the glass; to the fence; to the post with its old red twine; to the pair that makes the yard look held. "Thank you," I say. For this small deliverance. For the work I am still learning to do. For the way love can arrive with a tap and leave with a song and stay like heat in a kitchen where someone remembered to keep the kettle clean. I place a clean towel where a wet hand will want it and call that a hymn.

If there is doctrine, it fits on one line. Anchor first. Window after. We pass that line to visitors with a bowl and a spoon and point them to the post at dusk. Most understand. The rest learn by watching. The birds keep their hours. The town keeps its tune. I keep the frame dusted and the needle threaded. It is a good life for a man who once tried to outwait sorrow instead of outwork it.

North Carolina summer's made the town open its screens. People left latches cocked to the first catch, not the second. The couriers timed their taps for morning shade and the blue hour after supper. We learned to set a small saucer near the sill, not as bait, as respect. A token needs a place to land. Respect turned out to be the cheapest and most effective lure for goodness.

We held a Window Day because Nora said the town needed a holiday that could be made with a rag. We washed glass. We wrote anchors on index cards and taped them near latches. We rang the threshold bells once at noon and once at dusk. No speeches. A potluck with more bread than sense. Children made construction paper birds and taped them to fence posts. Johnny tuned his truck whistle to the two note call and taught three kids to hit it clean. The sound carried to the creek and back, a small loop of competence the day could rest on.

A courier delivered a scrap of red fabric to the high school custodian who had eaten lunch alone for twenty years. He brought it to the gym and tied it to the rope that raises the curtain. At the wrong hour that afternoon, he pulled the rope and opened the stage. Three students wandered in and practiced a song for no reason but joy. The custodian sat on a bleacher and cried alone and not alone. He anchored by inviting them to use the stage on Tuesdays. That was the program. Three chairs. One broom. A light left on. The song moved down the hall and cleaned the air without asking for a grant.

Bella stood at my sink and cut oranges for Nora. She had a folder from the State in her bag and did not take it out. "They want charts," she said.

"What will you give them?" I asked.

"A recipe," she said. "One cup naming. One cup listening. Half cup apology. Half cup rest. Add heat. Stir. Serve with bowls. No chart." She wrote it on the back of a form that asked for incident codes and left it under the magnet with the photograph of the serviceberry in leaf.

Later we walked Oak with a roll of twine and tied small knots at posts where taps had come often. Not markers. Reminders to look up. At dusk, the male and female couriers perched on the post and sang the line they keep for warm nights. Love does not ask for encores. It leaves a tune in the mouth. We whistled it down Oak and it came back from the creek on its own. A man on his porch lifted a glass. A child on a bike slowed and tried the two notes and got close. Close is enough for a start. The night kept the tune like a coin kept for bus fare.

We learned one more habit that month. We left a chair near the front door of each house with a card tucked under the seat. The card said, *Sit before you speak*. It saved us from three arguments and one foolish marriage proposal. It also made two good ones better because the sit turned nerves to heat you could use.

Mistakes came in summer's ease. Two doors stayed open too long and a person with a talent for drawing a crowd began to call every knock holy. She turned her porch into a stage and her tokens into props. She called it love. It was appetite. The town does not punish. It adjusts. Adjustment is our best answer to harm when the harm has not yet turned to cruelty.

We visited in pairs. We sat on her steps and asked anchors. "What did you promise before you opened," I asked. She said the couriers wanted to hear her speak. That is not an anchor. That is a thirst. Bella sat beside me and said a sentence I wrote down later in the blue notebook. "Love is not a microphone," she said. "It is a sink and a towel and a chair pulled close." The woman looked at the towel on her rail as if it were a new object.

We asked her to stop opening until she could name one act that cost her comfort and gave someone else rest. She argued. We waited. Two days later she brought casserole to a neighbor she disliked and did not tell anyone until he mentioned it at Nora's. The couriers returned to her sill quietly the next week with a bent nail that fit a hinge on a door that had squealed for months. The porch stage closed. The door swung clean. The woman sat in her kitchen and cried where nobody clapped. That counted as health.

The dusk courier tested me again. He sat on the sill and lifted his crest and did not tap. I said my anchor before I stepped near. "I will not make a person into a door," I said aloud, like a child practicing a catechism. I opened the window a handspan and kept my feet on the floor. Heat moved, not rushed, to the return. It stopped where my borders stood. Love pressed and did not spill. That was the lesson. You can keep truth without drowning in it. You can say "yes" and still have a hallway to walk down after.

Bella stayed for tea. She put her badge on the table and traced its edge with a fingertip as if learning its shape before she left it. "They want an index for the couriers," she said. "I want a table."

"You have one," I said.

She looked around my kitchen. The kettle. The towel. The chair pulled close. She smiled and put the badge in her pocket and did not clip it on the next morning. She came back with flour on her sleeve and a note for Nora about onions. The State called twice. She let it ring. Later she took the badge to her mother's house and set it in a dish beside the phone. Her mother nodded and said, "good, eat with your hands again." That was their version of a ceremony.

We added a practice at the fence table for the summer mistakes. Before you take a token, name one person who will be warmer because of what you do next. Write the name. Put the card under a stone. Come back after and move the stone to the other side. The stones walked slowly across the table all season. By fall, the path had worn the wood to a soft groove that fit the thumb. People traced it while they waited for the bell. The groove kept our ambition from running ahead of our skill.

Two houses on Hazel had faced each other for years like siblings in a long sulk. On the left, an older woman with a garden ruled by marigolds, square beds, lines stringed tight, labels in tidy script. On the right, a man and his small son and a grill he used in every season, smoke that smelled like cedar, laughter that stopped at the hedge. Their feud had no single start. A dog. A hedge. A word that landed wrong. They lived like people who share a fence with the past and refuse to look through the knot holes.

A courier left a jar ring on the left hand sill. A courier left a train stub on the right hand stoop. Small circles. Old paths. The woman held the ring and remembered canning summers with a sister in a kitchen that smelled like steam and vinegar and a radio. The man held the ticket and remembered a night train and a person he had followed north and then south and a promise he had kept until he broke it. The tokens did not accuse. They asked for a motion.

Anchors were simple and hard. The woman brought a jar of pickles to the man's steps and rang the bell. "For the boy," she said. Her voice had the crack a jar makes the first time you open it after years. The man brought over a scrap piece of cedar, planed and sanded, that fit the gap in her fence she had cursed for a decade. "For the dog", he said. He hung the cedar with two screws and did not brag when it sat flush.

They did not become friends. They became neighbors. That is the love most towns need. The dog stopped escaping. The boy learned to wave without scowling. The marigolds stayed, a stubborn border that now looked like a line of small suns instead of a wall. In the evening the man lifted the lid of the grill and held it so the wind did not blow smoke into the woman's kitchen. She cracked her window one inch and let soup steam join the air. That counted as a treaty.

The boy learned the two note whistle from Johnny and taught it to a friend. He whistled at the hedge and a male cardinal answered from the serviceberry with the flourish he kept for evening. The boy's eyes widened as if something had knocked at his window and asked for his name. He said his own name into his hands and laughed. He did not know he had anchored. He would learn later that joy can be a promise kept. He took a jar ring from the kitchen and wore it on a string. He did not tell anyone why. He did not have to.

At dusk, the woman left a chair by her gate. The man left a cup hook under the eave for a bell. These were small changes. They made a path. The couriers used it the next week and left a straight pin and a bent washer. The fence swung without squeal. The boy's name traveled clean across the gap when his father called him for supper. When I walked past on my way to Nora's, I heard the bell ring once and then stop. It sounded like a house catching its breath between old habits and new ones.

I wrote the two addresses on a card in the blue notebook under Fence table examples and added a line. *Delivered and anchored. Weather mild. Names spoken without harm. Hedge learning manners. Marigolds holding. Grill cooperating.* It read like a ledger kept by a person who had finally forgiven himself for needing records to believe what his eyes already saw.

Bella chose a room. She did not make a speech. She arrived at Nora's with her badge in a dish and set it under the counter by the flour and the cards that tracked who needed soup and who had returned a bowl. "I can read a chart", Nora said, taking the badge and the dish. "I prefer a list". She slid the badge behind a stack of index cards and put the dish to work under a slow drip. The drip stopped. The dish had found its level.

Bella took a job at the Pine Street shop two days a week. Hands on wood, brains on grain. She kept a desk in the back with the tidy label "Field," as if love were a place you had to walk to with boots. On other days she knocked on doors as herself and not as the State and reminded people to say their anchors before they opened. She wrote in the blue notebook and put it back in my freezer with care. Her handwriting steadied the pages. It steadied me.

We kept our practices. Index cards by latches. Bowls on racks. Quiet hours. Bells rung at thresholds for arrivals and returns. The ferrymen came less, and when they did, we opened for them with respect and closed afterwards with rest. The couriers came as the air cooled. Tokens landed like punctuation on a sentence we were still writing together. We learned where to place commas so the breath stayed in the line. We learned when to stop and when to let the thought run to the next table.

In the evening, I touch the glass with two fingers and feel the habit of heat the couriers taught the house to hold. The pair on the post do what they do without metaphor. He brings a seed. She takes it. They both watch for hawk shadow and drink at noon when the ring loosens. They sing a line we have learned and do not own. We borrow it and whistle it back to the creek. It returns when the bell moves once and then settles. I think of Talinda then. She would have leaned into the sink and said, "listen with your shoulders," and I would have pretended not to understand until she smiled.

On the day Bella left her badge, the dusk courier sat at the sill while we ate and said nothing. We said our names into our cups. We said the names we had kept. We said "thank you" to the glass, to the fence, to the post with its old red twine. I wrote one more line in the songs book before I wrapped it and slid it back among the peas. Delivered and anchored. Weather clear. Names spoken without harm. Kettle clicked. Bell moved. Pair present. Tune in the mouth. Badge retired to useful silence.

Bella walked home with flour on her sleeve again. She looked lighter, not smaller. Choice does that when it is honest. At her mother's, two chairs sat closer than before. They ate oranges and did not reach for a speech. The birds on the wire marked the hour with two notes. That was enough. Later she told me her mother had put the badge in a drawer with photographs and a thimble. That drawer had become a kind of altar made of tools, which is the only altar our town trusts.

CARDINAL SINS

Autumn set the edges. The maples let go. The serviceberry carried its thin leaves longer, stubborn and small. Couriers tapped at the blue hour. People learned to keep a saucer at the sill and a sentence on the tongue. Anchors came clean when rehearsed. The light left early and the town refused to call that a verdict. We called it a "cue."

We held a Night of Names. Nora made soup. We wrote names on cards and read them into steam. We did not count who was dead and who was living. We put all names on one table and let the bell ring once for each. Lydia brought a loaf with three braids. She said her boy's name, then three more. Timmy whistled the two note in the hall and half the room answered. The sound swelled and settled like a blanket everyone agreed to share.

A courier left a scrap of sheet music on the school counselor's window. She learned the tune and taught it to seven students who hated the word "choir." They sang in the stairwell where the acoustics cut the day in half. Three janitors clapped. One visitor cried. The anchor sat in the notes, not in any speech after. The counselor wrote on the back of the scrap and taped it to the staff room door. *Sit before you speak. Hum before you argue.* The door stopped catching at the top. The principal claimed he had fixed it. We let him.

Bella's mother came to dinner with her badge in her purse and put it on the table when no one asked. She said her other daughter's name once. Bella took her hand. The dusk courier sat on the sill and did nothing. That was the gift. Love was the quiet between sentences. We did not waste it with a plan. We ate, we washed, we stacked. When the bell rang we did not applaud the bell. We nodded to the hand that lifted it.

Later we walked home through a street that smelled like leaves and soup. The post behind my kitchen held the pair. He brought a seed. She took it. He added the flourish he saved for evening. She answered with the clean version. We kept our distance and learned by watching. The two notes travel best when you are not trying to make them mean more than they do. They already carry enough. I stood at the sink and said "Talinda," then the names of two people I owed calls. I called one. I wrote the other on a card and stuck it to the frame.

We added a small practice after the Night of Names. We wrote three names in our pockets and carried them for a week. One we would say in a kitchen. One we would say outdoors. One we would say into a bowl of water before bed. The order did not matter. The saying did. Water remembers what you ask it to. So does wood. So do hands.

Familiar harms returned in new clothes. A man began to call his demands "anchors." He opened for couriers without promising anything that cost him comfort. He pressed his tokens on people who did not want them. He said he was loving hard.

He was not.

He was taking.

He used the bell as a gong and the window as a stage. His house sounded like a store that never closes.

We went as a circle. Six of us. We sat in his kitchen. We asked him to speak one true thing and to name one act that gave rest to someone else. He could not at first. He tried more words. We waited. He tried fewer. Finally, he said, I am afraid to be quiet. It was a small admission. It was a start. He did not like the sound of his own honesty. He kept going anyway. That counted.

We left him four cards and a bell. One card for truth. One for apology. One for an hour of work for a neighbor with no speech about it. One for rest. "Ring for each," we said. He hung the bell by his door and moved like a man learning a new route. He rang once that night, then twice the next day. A courier left a bent washer on his sill. He fixed the hinge on his wife's door and did not announce it. The house shifted, not much, enough. His wife stood longer at the sink and hummed. That was the measure.

He tried to turn the bell into a show again and caught himself. He rang it once and whispered the name of a person he had wronged. No one else heard. That is the point. Two weeks later he came to Nora's to return a stack of bowls without being asked. He set them down and left a jar ring in the dish for tokens. He is not cured. Neither are we. *Practice is not a cure. It is a path.* Bella wrote that line on a card and left it at the fence table. I copied it twice and kept one in my wallet.

The dusk courier tested our circle the next week. It sat on my sill, crest high, eyes exact. We said our anchors aloud before anyone moved. "I will not make love a law. I will not open every window for a flood. I will not confuse attention with care." We kept the window shut. We kept the tune in the mouth. The room warmed anyway. That felt like progress. Later, we opened for a different knock and carried a chair two blocks. The chair arrived and the person who needed it sat. That felt like proof.

We added a boundary practice for the loud months. *Before you tell a story about a token, tell a story about a task. Before you ring your bell, touch your sink. If you cannot name the anchor, keep the window shut.* It made three porches quieter and gave the birds a reason to visit again without having to cut through applause.

We started a fence table. *Scrap cedar, borrowed sawhorses, a jar for notes.* People left their anchors there when they could not say them at home. They wrote a line and placed a token beside it if they had one. A button. A stitch of fabric. A jar ring. The couriers learned the spot and delivered there when a sill was too risky. Love likes options. It thrives when you offer it two honest doors and let it pick.

The first note said, *I will stop keeping score.* The second said, *I will bring a chair into the kitchen for my mother.* The third was a child's drawing of a pot and three bowls and a smiling face in a window. We did not translate. We put the tokens in the blue notebook to record and returned them to the fence for claim. The jar filled and emptied like a lung. The cedar took on a smell of oil and weather that made you want to put your hands flat and rest.

At dusk, a courier left a length of red twine there with a knot at one end. The knot matched the notch in the serviceberry stake that had begun to slip. Theo came by and tied the knot to the stake and the stake to the stem. The tree held straighter in the next wind. Little gains matter when the season turns. We took a picture for the notebook and wrote, *stake corrected, lesson noted.* The picture looked ordinary. That was the victory.

Mia added a line to the practice. *We pay for a token with one hour of quiet work.* She fixed a loose tread on the stairs in the church basement. No sign. No speech. The tread took weight without complaint that Sunday. That is love. Timmy adjusted a mirror at the corner by Kopek's that had been off by a finger for years. The street felt smarter by noon. Lydia set a bowl on the fence table with three slips. Names for someone who cannot speak today. The bowl emptied before supper.

By the end of the month the fence table had a patina. Coffee rings. Pencil smears. A knife mark where someone cut twine for a package and left the extra inch for the next person. We sanded nothing. We let the wear stand. The table taught without trying. People left fewer speeches and more verbs. "Folded shirts for my sister. Ride to the clinic for Mr. Han. Door oiled at 14 Willow." Anchors with addresses. The birds began to perch on the chair backs while we wrote. They did not read. They kept us honest. The sight of a red back at your elbow makes you think twice before you write a lie.

We learned to leave the table uncovered in rain. Paper warps, then dries, then holds ink better. The jar kept notes safe enough. The cedar swelled and relaxed. People trusted it more after it had survived a storm. That is how trust often works here. You watch a thing get wet and still be useful. You stop asking for guarantees you cannot give yourself.

Winter bit. Pipes trembled. The bus hissed and slid. The bell rang for arrivals and returns. We kept water warm at the dish and the feeder full. We learned the timing again. Noon thaw. Dusk freeze. The cardinals moved like experts. Two notes, then none. Drink, then hide. We counted not to hoard but to time our help.

A courier left a small brass screw on Ruth's father's sill. He had been cursing a loose leg on his table for a month. He used the screw and the leg held. He cried once, quietly, then laughed at his own tears. He called Ruth and told her the table stood like an old soldier and she said she would bring soup. He said he already had soup and would take bread. Anchors rarely fancy themselves. He put the screw card in the jar with the simple word done.

We organized room checks for the people who use words like 'I'm fine' too easily. Two knocks, then a word through the door. Anchor spoken aloud. Window closed or open with a promise named. It felt nosy. It felt like care. The dusk courier watched us from three sills that week and did not tap. We passed. The pass did not feel like a grade. It felt like a nod from a teacher who trusts you to show up again.

Timmy pulled two cars from drifts and refused money. He accepted a jar ring and a button and put both on his dash. Lydia burned a loaf and made another without cursing. Mia wrapped the shop pipes with old blankets cut into strips and taped a card to the door.

If your heat fails, come sit. We have chairs and steam. Nora kept a pot at a slow bubble from dawn to dusk and scolded anyone who tried to apologize for needing seconds.

The State tried again with a form. Bella brought it to Nora and slid it under the flour bin. Nora wrote a recipe on top of it and handed that back instead. *One onion. Two cloves garlic. One cup lentils. Three cups water. Salt. Heat. Bowls. Silence while eating. Conversation after.* The State sent a thank you that did not make sense and did not complain again that month. A clerk called to ask if the lentils were mandatory. Bella said "optional". The clerk laughed and hung up.

On the coldest morning the pair still found the ring of water at noon. They drank and lifted their heads between sips, the old blessing shape. The sight steadied my hands more than any chart could. We do not live by numbers here. We live by small timings and kept promises. I wrote *Talinda* on the fog of the glass and watched the letters fade. I did not feel bereft. I felt accompanied.

We kept a list by the fence table titled "Warm." We added names of houses that would host for an hour. We added kettles by size. We added the times when the noon ring was widest. The list made us feel like a town that had learned a song and could sing it without a conductor. The birds did their part. They arrived. They drank. They left us the small gift of a room that did not give up.

Spring returned, and with it the small rush. People cleaned windows. Couriers tapped. The fence table filled. We held Window Day again. Bells rang at noon and dusk. The town felt like a place that had been taught to breathe. The air had our tune in it. You could hear it in the way doors opened and shut.

The night after Window Day, the dusk courier came for me with a token I did not see. I said my anchor before my hand went to the latch. "I will ask for help before I break." I opened the window a handspan. Warmth moved. The bird sang the three that rise and fall. I felt my shoulders drop and my mouth soften. The token slid in, a single straight pin. I put it on the sill. I knew what it was for. A collar that has sat wrong for a year. A shirt I love that I refused to mend. A task I have avoided because avoiding distilled into pride. Pride is a brittle glue. Pins do better work.

I sewed the collar as the kettle clicked. Bella sat with oranges and read from the blue notebook while I stitched. Delivered and anchored. Weather cold and clear. Names spoken without harm. She added a line. Quiet held. Tune intact. She peeled an orange and set three pieces in a row. Eat, talk, rest. We ate, we talked, we rested. The pin held. The day did not ask for a poem. It asked for thread.

The next morning I took the mended shirt to the fence table and wrote, *ask for help when the seam fights back*. Three people copied it to their own cards. One came by that afternoon and asked for a ride to the doctor. We drove. We did not turn the radio on. We did not need to fill the car with noise. The card went back under the stone with a small crease where a thumb had pressed it. That crease felt like proof.

Outside, the pair on the post began the dawn song before the light got its grip on the fence. He brought a seed. She took it. Then she brought one to him. He took it. They did not owe a pattern to anyone watching. They practiced the trade until both looked fed. We listened through the glass without needing to make it more. Love had arrived enough times to be a habit. We kept the habit. We kept the tune. We kept a chair pulled close. We rang the bell when we left and when we returned. We said "thank you" to the glass and the post and the thin red twine that still marked the place where a different kind of knock had once announced the opposite work.

The couriers stayed as long as we kept our side. Anchors first. Windows after. Names into steam. Bowls on tables. The town went on. The serviceberry took its new shape. The fence table weathered and got better. The dusk courier came and left. We practiced until practice felt like love and love felt like practice. When the maples leafed, we did not say that the season had saved us. We said we had helped the season do its job. The birds agreed with two notes and a quiet that tasted like rest.

That evening, I put on the mended shirt and stood at the sink and said "Talinda," clear, round, like a bell you keep for rain. The glass held my palm. The heat answered with the steadiness of a house that has learned its people. The pair on the post ran their line and did not look in. Love does not need to check its work when the work has become the room. I wrote one more card and tucked it under the frame. *Keep the kettle clean. Keep the towel dry. Keep the bell honest.* Then I turned off the lamp, let the tune sit in the dark, and trusted the window to remember what to do at dawn.

www.ingramcontent.com/pod-product-compliance
Lightning Source LLC
LaVergne TN
LVHW041632070526
838199LV00052B/3317